The Book of
PIRATES

Also selected and illustrated by Michael Hague

THE BOOK OF DRAGONS

THE BOOK OF FAIRIES

The Book of
PIRATES

SELECTED AND ILLUSTRATED BY
MICHAEL HAGUE

HarperCollins*Publishers*

The Book of Pirates
Copyright © 2001 by Michael Hague
Printed in the United States of America.
All rights reserved.
www.harperchildrens.com

Library of Congress Cataloging-in-Publication Data
The book of pirates / selected and illustrated by Michael Hague.— 1st ed.
p.   cm.
Contents: "Oh, better far to live and die," from The pirates of Penzance / Gilbert and Sullivan — From The master of Ballantrae
/ Robert Louis Stevenson — Captain Sharkey, How the Governor of Saint Kitt's came home / Arthur Conan Doyle — "The
island come true," from Peter Pan / J. M. Barrie — "The rebels-convict," from Captain Blood / Rafael Sabatini — A ballad of
John Silver / John Masefield — "The reformed pirate" / Frank Stockton — The female smuggler / collected by W. B. Whall —
Wolfert Webber, or Golden dreams / Washington Irving — Lyrics from The Buccaneer / John Masefield — "Tom Chist and the
treasure box," from Tales of pirates and buccaneers / Howard Pyle.
ISBN 0-688-14003-3
I. Pirates—Literary collections. [1. Pirates—Literary collections.] I. Hague, Michael.
PZ5.B6428 2001   00-053541
808.8'035291—dc21   CIP
                                                                                                                                                      AC

10   9   8   7   6   5   4   3   2   1

First Edition

This book is dedicated to the men and boys of the Flower City and the Stat Geeks League. A more ruthless band of cutthroats, thieves, and thugs has never roamed the open seas.

Special thanks to Josh Weiss for his contributions to this book.

Contents

"Oh, Better Far to Live and Die" from *The Pirates of Penzance*

Gilbert and Sullivan

King:

Oh, better far to live and die
Under the brave black flag I fly,
Than play a sanctimonious part
With a pirate head and a pirate heart.
Away to the cheating world go you,
Where pirates all are well-to-do;
But I'll be true to the song I sing,
And live and die a Pirate King.

   For I am a Pirate King!
And it is, it is a glorious thing
To be a Pirate King!
   For I am a Pirate King!

All:
  You are!
Hurrah for the Pirate King!

King:
And it is, it is a glorious thing
To be a Pirate King.

All:
  It is!
Hurrah for the Pirate King!
Hurrah for the Pirate King!

King:
When I sally forth to seek my prey
I help myself in a royal way.
I sink a few more ships, it's true,
Than a well-bred monarch ought to do;
But many a king on a first-class throne,
If he wants to call his crown his own,
Must manage somehow to get through
More dirty work than e'er *I* do,
  For I am a Pirate King!
And it is, it is a glorious thing
To be a Pirate King!
  For I am a Pirate King!

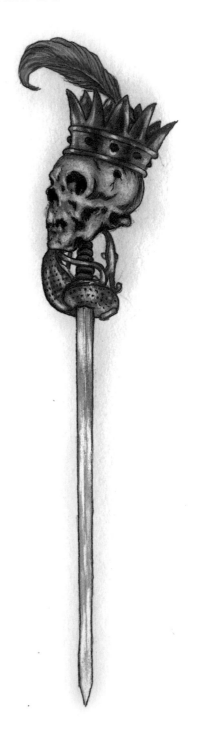

All:
  You are!
Hurrah for the Pirate King!

King:
And it is, it is a glorious thing
To be a Pirate King.

All:
  It is!
Hurrah for the Pirate King!
Hurrah for the Pirate King!

From *The Master of Ballantrae*

Robert Louis Stevenson

The ship was very old; and the skipper, although the most honest of men, was one of the least capable. The wind blew very boisterous, and the sea raged extremely. All that day we had little heart whether to eat or drink; went early to rest in some concern of mind; and (as if to give us a lesson) in the night the wind chopped suddenly into the northeast, and blew a hurricane. We were awaked by the dreadful thunder of the tempest and the stamping of the mariners on deck; so that I supposed our last hour was certainly come; and the terror of my mind was increased out of all measure by Ballantrae, who mocked at my devotions. For three days we lay in the dark in the cabin, and had but a biscuit to nibble. On the fourth the wind fell, leaving the ship dismasted and heaving on vast billows. The captain had not a guess of whither we were blown; he was stark ignorant of his trade, and could do naught but bless the Holy Virgin; a very good thing, too, but scarce the whole of seamanship. It seemed our one hope was to be picked up by another vessel.

The fifth and sixth days we tossed there helpless. The seventh some sail was got on her, but she was an unwieldy vessel at the best, and we made little but leeway. All the time, indeed, we had been drifting to the south and west, and during the tempest must have driven in that direction with unheard-of violence. The ninth dawn was cold and black, with a great sea running, and every mark of foul weather. In this situation we were overjoyed to sight a small ship on the horizon, and to perceive her go about and head for the *Sainte-Marie*. But our gratification did not very long endure; for when she had laid to and lowered a boat, it was immediately filled with disorderly fellows, who sang and shouted as they pulled across to us, and swarmed in on our deck with bare cutlasses, cursing loudly. Their leader was a horrible villain, with his face blacked and his whiskers curled in ringlets; Teach, his name; a most notorious pirate. He stamped about the deck, raving and crying out that his name was Satan, and his ship was called Hell. There was something about him like a wicked child or a half-witted person, that daunted me beyond expression. I whispered in the ear of Ballantrae that I would not be the last to volunteer, and only prayed God they might be short of hands; he approved my purpose with a nod.

"Bedad," said I to Master Teach, "if you are Satan, here is a devil for ye."

The word pleased him; and (not to dwell upon these shocking incidents) Ballantrae and I and two others were taken for recruits, while the skipper and all the rest were cast into the sea by the method of walking the plank. It was the first time I had seen this done; my heart died within me at the spectacle; and Master Teach or one of his acolytes (for my head was too much lost to be precise) remarked upon my pale face in a very alarming manner. I had

the strength to cut a step or two of a jig, and cry out some ribaldry, which saved me for that time; but my legs were like water when I must get down into the skiff among these miscreants; and what with my horror of my company and fear of the monstrous billows, it was all I could do to keep an Irish tongue and break a jest or two as we were pulled aboard. By the blessing of God, there was a fiddle in the pirate ship, which I had no sooner seen than I fell upon; and in my quality of crowder I had the heavenly good luck to get favor in their eyes. Crowding Pat was the name they dubbed me with; and it was little I cared for a name so long as my skin was whole.

What kind of a pandemonium that vessel was, I cannot describe, but she was commanded by a lunatic, and might be called a floating Bedlam. Drinking, roaring, singing, quarreling, dancing, they were never all sober at one time; and there were days together when, if a squall had supervened, it must have sent us to the bottom; or if a king's ship had come along, it would have found us quite helpless for defense. Once or twice we sighted a sail, and, if we were sober enough, overhauled her, God forgive us! and if we were all too drunk, she got away, and I would bless the saints under my breath. Teach ruled, if you can call that rule which brought no order, by the terror he created; and I observed the man was very vain of his position. I have known marshals of France—ay, and even Highland chieftains—that were less openly puffed up; which throws a singular light on the pursuit of honor and glory.

It was long before I got private speech of Ballantrae; but at length one night we crept out upon the bowsprit, when the rest were better employed, and commiserated our position.

"None can deliver us but the saints," said I.

"My mind is very different," said Ballantrae; "for I am going to deliver myself. This Teach is the poorest creature possible; we make no profit of him, and lie continually open to capture; and," says he, "I am not going to be a tarry pirate for nothing, nor yet to hang in chains if I can help it." And he told me what was in his mind to better the state of the ship in the way of discipline, which would give us safety for the present, and a sooner hope of deliverance when they should have gained enough and should break up their company.

I confessed to him ingenuously that my nerve was quite shook amid these horrible surroundings, and I durst scarce tell him to count upon me.

"I am not very easily frightened," said he, "nor very easily beat."

A few days after, there befell an accident which had nearly hanged us all; and offers the most extraordinary picture of the folly that ruled in our concerns. We were all pretty drunk: and some bedlamite spying a sail, Teach put the ship about in chase without a glance, and we began to bustle up the arms and boast of the horrors that should follow. I observed Ballantrae stood quiet in the bows, looking under the shade of his hand; but for my part, true to my policy among these savages, I was at work with the busiest and passing Irish jests for their diversion.

"Run up the colors," cries Teach. "Show the —s the Jolly Roger!"

It was the merest drunken braggadocio at such a stage, and might have lost us a valuable prize; but I thought it no part of mine to reason, and I ran up the black flag with my own hand.

Ballantrae steps presently aft with a smile upon his face.

"You may perhaps like to know, you drunken dog," says he, "that you are chasing a king's ship."

Teach roared him the lie; but he ran at the same time to the bulwarks, and so did they all. I have never seen so many drunken men struck suddenly sober. The cruiser had gone about, upon our impudent display of colors; she was just then filling on the new tack; her ensign blew out quite plain to see; and even as we stared, there came a puff of smoke, and then a report, and a shot plunged in the waves a good way short of us. Some ran to the ropes, and got the *Sarah* round with an incredible swiftness. One fellow fell on the rum barrel, which stood broached upon the deck, and rolled it promptly overboard. On my part, I made for the Jolly Roger, struck it, tossed it in the sea; and could have flung myself after, so vexed was I with our mismanagement.

As for Teach, he grew as pale as death, and incontinently went down to his cabin. Only twice he came on deck that afternoon; went to the taffrail; took a long look at the king's ship, which was still on the horizon heading after us; and then, without speech, back to his cabin. You may say he deserted us; and if it had not been for one very capable sailor we had on board and for the lightness of the airs that blew all day, we must certainly have gone to the yardarm.

It is to be supposed Teach was humiliated, and perhaps alarmed for his position with the crew; and the way in which he set about regaining what he had lost, was highly characteristic of the man. Early next day we smelled him burning sulphur in his cabin and crying out, "Hell, hell!" which was well understood among the crew, and filled their minds with apprehension. Presently he comes on deck, a perfect figure of fun, his face blacked, his hair and whiskers curled, his belt stuck full of pistols; chewing bits of glass so that the blood ran down his chin, and brandishing a dirk. I do not know if he had taken these manners from the Indians of America, where he was a native; but such was his way, and he would always thus announce that he was wound up to horrid deeds. The first that came near him was the fellow who had sent the rum overboard the day before; him he stabbed to the heart, damning him for a mutineer; and then capered about the body, raving and swearing and daring us to come on. It was the silliest exhibition; and yet dangerous too, for the cowardly fellow was plainly working himself up to another murder.

All of a sudden Ballantrae stepped forth. "Have done with this play-acting," says he. "Do you think to frighten us with making faces? We saw nothing of you yesterday, when you were wanted; and we did well without you, let me tell you that."

There was a murmur and a movement in the crew, of pleasure and alarm, I thought, in nearly equal parts. As for Teach, he gave a barbarous howl, and swung his dirk to fling it, an art in which (like many seamen) he was very expert.

"Knock that out of his hand!" says Ballantrae, so sudden and sharp that my arm obeyed him before my mind had understood.

Teach stood like one stupid, never thinking on his pistols.

"Go down to your cabin," cries Ballantrae, "and come on deck again when you are sober. Do you think we are going to hang for you, you half-witted, drunken brute and butcher? Go down!" And he stamped his foot at him with such a sudden smartness that Teach fairly ran for it to the companion.

"And, now mates," says Ballantrae, "a word with you. I don't know if you are gentlemen of fortune for the fun of the thing, but I am not. I want to make money, and get ashore again, and spend it like a man. And on one thing my mind is made up: I will not hang if I can help it. Come: give me a hint; I'm only a beginner! Is there no way to get a little discipline and common sense about this business?"

One of the men spoke up: he said by rights they should have a quartermaster; and no sooner was the word out of his mouth than they were all of that opinion. The thing went by acclamation, Ballantrae was made quartermaster, the rum was put in his charge, laws were passed in imitation of those of a pirate by the name of Roberts, and the last proposal was to make an end of Teach. But Ballantrae was afraid of a more efficient captain, who might be a counterweight to himself, and he opposed this stoutly. Teach, he said, was good enough to board ships and to frighten fools with his blacked face and swearing; we could scarce get a better man than Teach for that; and besides, as the man was now disconsidered and as good as deposed, we might reduce his proportion of the plunder. This carried it; Teach's share was cut down to a mere derision, being actually less than mine; and there remained only two points: whether he would consent, and who was to announce to him this resolution.

"Do not let that stick you," says Ballantrae. "I will do that."

And he stepped to the companion and down alone into the cabin to face the drunken savage.

"This is the man for us," cries one of the hands. "Three cheers for that quartermaster!" which were given with a will, my own voice among the loudest, and I dare say these plaudits had their effect on Master Teach in the cabin.

What passed precisely was never known, though some of the heads of it came to the surface later on; and we were all amazed, as well as gratified, when Ballantrae came on deck with Teach upon his arm, and announced that all had been consented.

I pass swiftly over those twelve or fifteen months in which we continued to keep the sea in the North Atlantic, getting our food and water from the ships we overhauled, and doing on the whole a pretty fortunate business. Sure, no one could wish to read anything so ungenteel as the memoirs of a pirate, even an unwilling one like me! Things went extremely better with our designs, and Ballantrae kept his lead, to my admiration, from that day forth. I would be tempted to suppose that a gentleman must everywhere be first, even aboard a rover: but my birth is every whit as good as any Scottish lord's, and I am not ashamed to confess that I stayed Crowding Pat until the end, and was not much better than the crew's buffoon. Indeed, it was no scene to bring out my merits.

My health suffered from a variety of reasons; I was more at home to the last on a horse's back than a ship's deck; and, to be ingenuous, the fear of the sea was constantly in my mind, battling with the fear of my companions.

I need not cry myself up for courage; I have done well on many fields under the eyes of famous generals, and earned my late advancement by an act of the most distinguished valor before many witnesses. But when we must proceed on one of our abordages, the heart of Francis Burke was in his boots; the little eggshell skiff in which we must set forth, the horrible heaving of the vast billows, the height of the ship that we must scale, the thought of how many there might be there in garrison upon their legitimate defense, the scowling heavens which (in that climate) so often looked darkly down upon our exploits, and the mere crying of the wind in my ears, were all considerations most unpalatable to my valor. Besides which, as I was always a creature of the nicest sensibility, the scenes that must follow on our success tempted me as little as the chances of defeat. Twice we found women on board; and though I have seen towns sacked, and of late days in France some very horrid public tumults, there was something in the smallness of the numbers engaged, and the bleak, dangerous sea-surroundings, that made these acts of piracy far the most revolting.

I confess ingenuously I could never proceed unless I was three parts drunk; it was the same even with the crew; Teach himself was fit for no enterprise till he was full of rum; and it was one of the most difficult parts of Ballantrae's performance, to serve us with liquor in the proper quantities. Even this he did to admiration; being upon the whole the most capable man I ever met with, and the one of the most natural genius. He did not even scrape favor with the crew, as I did, by continual buffoonery made upon a very anxious heart; but preserved on most occasions a great deal of gravity and distance: so that he was like a parent among a family of young children, or a schoolmaster with his boys. What made his part the harder to perform, the men were inveterate grumblers; Ballantrae's discipline, little as it was, was yet irksome to their love of license: and what was worse, being kept sober they had time to think. Some of them accordingly would fall to repenting their abominable crimes; one in particular, who was a good Catholic, and with whom I would sometimes steal apart for prayer; above all in bad weather, fogs, lashing rain, and the like, when we would be the less observed; and I am sure no two criminals in the cart have ever performed their devotions with more anxious sincerity.

But the rest, having no such grounds of hope, fell to another pastime, that of computation. All day long they would be telling up their shares or glooming over the result. I have said we were pretty fortunate. But an observation falls to be made: that in this world, in no business that I have tried, do the profits rise to a man's expectations. We found many ships and took many; yet few of them contained much money, their goods were usually nothing to our purpose—what did we want with a cargo of ploughs, or even of tobacco?—and it is quite a painful reflection how many whole crews we have made to walk the plank for no more than a stock of biscuits or an anker or two of spirits.

In the meanwhile our ship was growing very foul, and it was high time we should make for our *port de carénage*, which was in the estuary of a river among swamps. It was openly understood that we should then break up and go and squander our proportions of the spoil; and this made every man greedy of a little more, so that our decision was delayed from day to day. What finally decided matters was a trifling accident, such as an ignorant person might suppose incidental to our way of life. But here I must explain: on only one of all the ships we boarded, the first on which we found women, did we meet with any genuine resistance. On that occasion we had two men killed and several injured, and if it had not been for the gallantry of Ballantrae we had surely been beat back at last. Everywhere else the defense (where there was any at all) was what the worst troops in Europe would have laughed at; so that the most dangerous part of our employment was to clamber up the side of the ship; and I have even known the poor souls on board to cast us a line, so eager were they to volunteer instead of walking the plank.

This constant immunity had made our fellows very soft, so that I understood how Teach had made so deep a mark upon their minds; for indeed the company of that lunatic was the chief danger in our way of life. The accident to which I have referred was this: We had sighted a little full-rigged ship very close under our board in a haze; she sailed near as well as we did; I should be nearer truth if I said, near as ill; and we cleared the bowchaser to see if we could bring a spar or two about their ears. The swell was exceeding great; the motion of the ship beyond description; it was little wonder if our gunners should fire thrice and be still quite broad of what they aimed at. But in the meanwhile the chase had cleared a stern gun, the thickness of the air concealing them; and being better marksmen, their first shot struck us in the bows, knocked our two gunners into mincemeat, so that we were all sprinkled with the blood, and plunged through the deck into the forecastle, where we slept.

Ballantrae would have held on; indeed, there was nothing in this *contretemps* to affect the mind of any soldier; but he had a quick perception of the men's wishes, and it was plain this lucky shot had given them a sickener of their trade. In a moment they were all of one mind: the chase was drawing away from us, it was needless to hold on, the *Sarah* was too foul to overhaul a bottle, it was mere foolery to keep the sea with her; and on these pretended grounds her head was incontinently put about and the course laid for the river. It was strange to see what merriment fell on that ship's company, and how they stamped about the deck jesting, and each computing what increase had come to his share by the death of the two gunners.

We were nine days making our port, so light were the airs we had to sail on, so foul was the ship's bottom; but early on the tenth, before dawn, and in a light lifting haze, we passed the head. A little after, the haze lifted, and fell again, showing us a cruiser very close. This was a sore blow, happening so near our refuge. There was a great debate of whether she had seen us, and if so whether it was likely they had recognized the *Sarah*. We were very careful, by destroying every member of those crews we overhauled, to leave no evidence as to our own persons; but the appearance of the *Sarah* herself we could not keep so private: and above all of late, since she had been foul, and we had pursued many ships without success, it was plain that her description had been often published.

I supposed this alert would have made us separate upon the instant. But here again that original genius of Ballantrae's had a surprise in store for me. He and Teach (and it was the most remarkable step of his success) had gone hand in hand since the first day of his appointment. I often questioned him upon the fact, and never got an answer but once, when he told me he and Teach had an understanding "which would very much surprise the crew if they should hear of it, and would surprise himself a good deal if it was carried out." Well, here again he and Teach were of a mind; and by their joint procurement the anchor was no sooner down than the whole crew went off upon a scene of drunkenness indescribable. By afternoon we were a mere shipful of lunatical persons, throwing of things overboard, howling of different songs at the same time, quarreling and falling together, and then forgetting our quarrels to embrace. Ballantrae had bid me drink nothing, and feign drunkenness, as I valued my life; and I have never passed a day so wearisomely, lying the best part of the time upon the forecastle and watching the swamps and thickets by which our little basin was entirely surrounded for the eye.

A little after dusk Ballantrae stumbled up to my side, feigned to fall, with a drunken laugh, and before he got his feet again, whispered me to "reel down into the cabin and seem to fall asleep upon a locker, for there would be need of me soon." I did as I was told, and coming into the cabin, where it was quite dark, let myself fall on the first locker. There was a man there already; by the way he stirred and threw me off, I could not think he was much in liquor; and yet when I had found another place, he seemed to continue to sleep on. My heart now beat very hard, for I saw some desperate matter was in act. Presently down came Ballantrae, lit the lamp, looked about the cabin, nodded as if pleased, and on deck again without a word. I peered out from between my fingers, and saw there were three of us slumbering, or feigning to slumber, on the lockers: myself, one Dutton and one Grady, both resolute men. On deck the rest were got to a pitch of revelry quite beyond the bounds of what is human; so that no reasonable name can describe the sounds they were now making. I have heard many a drunken bout in my time, many on board that very *Sarah*, but never anything the least like this, which made me early suppose the liquor had been tampered with. It was a long while before these yells and howls died out into a sort of miserable moaning, and then to silence; and it seemed a long while after that before Ballantrae came down again, this time with Teach upon his heels. The latter cursed at the sight of us three upon the lockers.

"Tut," says Ballantrae, "you might fire a pistol at their ears. You know what stuff they have been swallowing."

There was a hatch in the cabin floor, and under that the richest part of the booty was stored against the day of division. It fastened with a ring and three padlocks, the keys (for greater security) being divided; one to Teach, one to Ballantrae, and one to the mate, a man called Hammond. Yet I was amazed to see they were now all in the one hand; and yet more amazed (still looking through my fingers) to observe Ballantrae and Teach bring up several packets, four of them in all, very carefully made up and with a loop for carriage.

"And now," says Teach, "let us be going."

"One word," says Ballantrae. "I have discovered there is another man

besides yourself who knows a private path across the swamp; and it seems it is shorter than yours."

Teach cried out, in that case, they were undone.

"I do not know for that," says Ballantrae. "For there are several other circumstances with which I must acquaint you. First of all, there is no bullet in your pistols, which (if you remember) I was kind enough to load for both of us this morning. Secondly, as there is someone else who knows a passage, you must think it highly improbable I should saddle myself with a lunatic like you. Thirdly, these gentlemen (who need no longer pretend to be asleep) are those of my party, and will now proceed to gag and bind you to the mast; and when your men awaken (if they ever do awake after the drugs we have mingled in their liquor), I am sure they will be so obliging as to deliver you, and you will have no difficulty, I daresay, to explain the business of the keys."

Not a word said Teach, but looked at us like a frightened baby as we gagged and bound him.

"Now you see, you moon-calf," says Ballantrae, "why we make four packets. Heretofore you have been called Captain Teach, but I think you are now rather Captain Learn."

"Captain Sharkey: How the Governor of Saint Kitt's Came Home"

Arthur Conan Doyle

When the great wars of the Spanish Succession had been brought to an end by the Treaty of Utrecht, the vast number of privateers which had been fitted out by the contending parties found their occupation gone. Some took to the more peaceful but less lucrative ways of ordinary commerce, others were absorbed into the fishing fleets, and a few of the more reckless hoisted the Jolly Roger at the mizzen and the bloody flag at the main, declaring a private war upon their own account against the whole human race.

With mixed crews recruited from every nation, they scoured the seas, disappearing occasionally to careen in some lonely inlet, or putting in for a debauch at some outlying port, where they dazzled the inhabitants by their lavishness and horrified them by their brutalities.

On the Coromandel Coast, at Madagascar, in the African waters, and above all in the West Indian and American seas, the pirates were a constant menace. With an insolent luxury they would regulate their depredations by the comfort of the seasons, harrying New England in the summer and dropping south again to the tropical islands in the winter.

They were the more to be dreaded because they had none of that discipline and restraint which made their predecessors, the Buccaneers, both formidable and respectable. These Ishmaels of the sea rendered an account to no man, and treated their prisoners according to the drunken whim of the moment. Flashes of grotesque generosity alternated with longer stretches of inconceivable ferocity, and the skipper who fell into their hands might find himself dismissed with his cargo, after serving as boon companion in some hideous debauch, or might sit at his cabin table with his own nose and his lips served up with pepper and salt in front of him. It took a stout seaman in those days to ply his calling in the Caribbean Gulf.

Such a man was Captain John Scarrow, of the ship *Morning Star*, and yet he breathed a long sigh of relief when he heard the splash of the falling anchor and swung at his moorings within a hundred yards of the guns of the citadel of Basseterre. St. Kitt's was his final port of call, and early next morning his bowsprit would be pointed for Old England. He had had enough of those robber-haunted seas. Ever since he had left Maracaibo upon the Main, with his full lading of sugar and red pepper, he had winced at every topsail which glimmered over the violet edge of the tropical sea. He had coasted up the Windward Islands, touching here and there, and assailed continually by stories of villainy and outrage.

Captain Sharkey, of the twenty-gun pirate barque *Happy Delivery*, had passed down the coast and had littered it with gutted vessels and with murdered men. Dreadful anecdotes were current of his grim pleasantries and of his inflexible ferocity. From the Bahamas to the Main his coal-black barque, with the ambiguous name, had been freighted with death and many things which are worse than death. So nervous was Captain Scarrow, with his new full-rigged ship and her full and valuable lading, that he struck out to the west as far as Bird's Island to be out of the usual track of commerce. And yet even in those solitary waters he had been unable to shake off sinister traces of Captain Sharkey.

One morning they had raised a single skiff adrift upon the face of the ocean. Its only occupant was a delirious seaman, who yelled hoarsely as they hoisted him aboard and showed a dried-up tongue like a black and wrinkled fungus at the back of his mouth. Water and nursing soon transformed him into the strongest and smartest sailor on the ship. He was from Marblehead, in New England, it seemed, and was the sole survivor of a schooner, which had been scuttled by the dreadful Sharkey.

For a week Hiram Evanson, for that was his name, had been adrift beneath a tropical sun. Sharkey had ordered the mangled remains of his late captain to be thrown into the boat, "as provisions for the voyage," but the seaman had at once committed them to the deep, lest the temptation should be more than he could bear. He had lived upon his own huge frame, until, at the last moment, the *Morning Star* had found him in that madness which is the precursor of such a death. It was no bad find for Captain Scarrow, for, with a short-handed crew, such a seaman as this big New Englander was a prize worth having. He vowed that he was the only man whom Captain Sharkey had ever placed under an obligation.

Now that they lay under the guns of Basseterre, all danger from the pirate was at an end, and yet the thought of him lay heavily upon the seaman's mind as he watched the agent's boat shooting out from the custom-house quay.

"I'll lay you a wager, Morgan," said he to the first mate, "that the agent will speak of Sharkey in the first hundred words that pass his lips."

"Well, captain, I'll have you a silver dollar, and chance it," said the rough old Bristol man beside him.

The African rowers shot the boat alongside, and the linen-clad steersman sprang up the ladder.

"Welcome, Captain Scarrow!" he cried. "Have you heard about Sharkey."

The captain grinned at the mate.

"What devilry has he been up to now?" he asked.

"Devilry! You've not heard, then! Why, we've got him safe under lock and key here at Basseterre. He was tried last Wednesday, and he is to be hanged tomorrow morning."

Captain and mate gave a shout of joy, which an instant later was taken up by the crew. Discipline was forgotten as they scrambled up through the break of the poop to hear the news. The New Englander was in the front of them with a radiant face turned up to heaven, for he came of the Puritan stock.

"Sharkey to be hanged!" he cried. "You don't know, Master Agent, if they lack a hangman, do you?"

"Stand back!" cried the mate, whose outraged sense of discipline was even stronger than his interest at the news. "I'll pay that dollar, Captain Scarrow, with the lightest heart that ever I paid a wager yet. How came the villain to be taken?"

"Why, as to that, he became more than his own comrades could abide, and they took such a horror of him that they would not have him on the ship. So they marooned him upon the Little Mangles to the south of the Mysteriosa Bank, and there he was found by a Portobello trader, who brought him in. There was talk of sending him to Jamaica to be tried, but our good little governor, Sir Charles Ewan, would not hear of it. 'He's my meat,' said he, 'and I claim the cooking of it.' If you can stay till tomorrow morning at ten, you'll see the joint swinging."

"I wish I could," said the captain, wistfully, "but I am sadly behind time now. I should start with the evening tide."

"That you can't do," said the agent with decision. "The Governor is going back with you."

"The Governor!"

"Yes. He's had a dispatch from Government to return without delay. The flyboat that brought it has gone on to Virginia. So Sir Charles has been waiting for you, as I told him you were due before the rains."

"Well, well!" cried the captain, in some perplexity, "I'm a plain seaman, and I don't know much of governors and baronets and their ways. I don't remember that I even so much as spoke to one. But if it's in King George's service, and he asks a cast in the *Morning Star* as far as London, I'll do what I can for him. There's my own cabin he can have and welcome. As to the cooking, it's lobscouse and salmagundy six days in the week; but he can bring his own cook aboard with him if he thinks our galley too rough for his taste."

"You need not trouble your mind, Captain Scarrow," said the agent. "Sir Charles is in weak health just now, only clear of a quartan ague, and it is likely he will keep his cabin most of the voyage. Dr. Larousse said that he would have sunk had the hanging of Sharkey not put fresh life into him. He has a great spirit in him, though, and you must not blame him if he is somewhat short in his speech."

"He may say what he likes and do what he likes so long as he does not come athwart my hawse when I am working the ship," said the captain. "He is Governor of St. Kitt's, but I am Governor of the *Morning Star*. And, by his leave, I must weigh with the first tide, for I owe a duty to my employer, just as he does to King George."

"He can scarce be ready tonight, for he has many things to set in order before he leaves."

"The early morning tide, then."

"Very good. I shall send his things aboard tonight, and he will follow them tomorrow early if I can prevail upon him to leave St. Kitt's without seeing Sharkey do the rogue's hornpipe. His own orders were instant, so it may be that he will come at once. It is likely that Dr. Larousse may attend him upon the journey."

Left to themselves, the captain and mate made the best preparations which they could for their illustrious passenger. The largest cabin was turned out and adorned in his honor, and orders were given by which barrels of fruit and some cases of wine should be brought off to vary the plain food of an oceangoing trader. In the evening the Governor's baggage began to arrive—great ironbound ant-proof trunks, and official tin packing-cases, with other strange-shaped packages, which suggested the cocked hat or the sword within. And then there came a note, with a heraldic device upon the big red seal, to say that Sir Charles Ewan made his compliments to Captain Scarrow, and that he hoped to be with him in the morning as early as his duties and his infirmities would permit.

He was as good as his word, for the first gray of dawn had hardly begun to deepen into pink when he was brought alongside, and climbed with some difficulty up the ladder. The captain had heard that the Governor was an eccentric, but he was hardly prepared for the curious figure who came limping feebly down his quarterdeck, his steps supported by a thick bamboo cane. He wore a Ramillies wig, all twisted into little tails like a poodle's coat, and cut so low across the brow that the large green glasses which covered his eyes looked as if they were hung from it. A fierce beak of a nose, very long and very thin, cut the air in front of him. His ague had caused him to swathe his throat and chin with a broad linen cravat, and he wore a loose damask powdering-gown secured by a cord round the waist. As he advanced, he carried his masterful nose high in the air, but his head turned slowly from side to side in the helpless manner of the purblind, and he called in a high, querulous voice for the captain.

"You have my things?" he asked.

"Yes, Sir Charles."

"Have you wine aboard?"

"I have ordered five cases, sir."

"And tobacco?"

"There is a keg of Trinidad."

"You play a hand at piquet?"

"Passably well, sir."

"Then up anchor, and to sea!"

There was a fresh westerly wind, so by the time the sun was fairly through the morning haze, the ship was hull down from the islands. The decrepit Governor still limped the deck, with one guiding hand upon the quarter rail.

"You are on Government service now, captain," said he. "They are counting the days till I come to Westminster, I promise you. Have you all that she will carry?"

"Every inch, Sir Charles."

"Keep her so if you blow the sails out of her. I fear, Captain Scarrow, that you will find a blind and broken man a poor companion for your voyage."

"I am honored in enjoying your Excellency's society," said the captain. "But I am sorry that your eyes should be so afflicted."

"Yes, indeed. It is the cursed glare of the sun on the white streets of Basseterre which has gone far to burn them out."

"I had heard also that you had been plagued by a quartan ague."

"Yes; I have had a pyrexy, which has reduced me much."

"We had set aside a cabin for your surgeon."

"Ah, the rascal! There was no budging him, for he has a snug business amongst the merchants. But hark!"

He raised his ring-covered hand in the air. From far astern there came the low deep thunder of cannon.

"It is from the island!" cried the captain in astonishment. "Can it be a signal for us to put back?"

The Governor laughed.

"You have heard that Sharkey, the pirate, is to be hanged this morning. I ordered the batteries to salute when the rascal was kicking his last, so that I might know of it out at sea. There's an end of Sharkey!"

"There's an end of Sharkey!" cried the captain; and the crew took up the cry as they gathered in little knots upon the deck and stared back at the low, purple line of the vanishing land.

It was a cheering omen for their start across the Western Ocean, and the invalid Governor found himself a popular man on board, for it was generally understood that but for his insistence upon an immediate trial and sentence, the villain might have played upon some more venal judge and so escaped. At dinner that day Sir Charles gave many anecdotes of the deceased pirate; and so affable was he, and so skillful in adapting his conversation to men of lower degree, that captain, mate, and Governor smoked their long pipes and drank their claret as three good comrades should.

"And what figure did Sharkey cut in the dock?" asked the captain.

"He is a man of some presence," said the Governor.

"I had always understood that he was an ugly, sneering devil," remarked the mate.

"Well, I dare say he could look ugly upon occasions," said the Governor.

"I have heard a New Bedford whaleman say that he could not forget his eyes," said Captain Scarrow. "They were of the lightest filmy blue, with red-rimmed lids. Was that not so, Sir Charles?"

"Alas, my own eyes will not permit me to know much of those of others! But I remember now that the Adjutant-General said that he had such an eye as you describe, and added that the jury were so foolish as to be visibly discomposed when it was turned upon them. It is well for them that he is dead, for he was a man who would never forget an injury, and if he had laid hands upon any one of them he would have stuffed him with straw and hung him for a figurehead."

The idea seemed to amuse the Governor, for he broke suddenly into a high, neighing laugh, and the two seamen laughed also, but not so heartily, for they remembered that Sharkey was not the last pirate who sailed the western seas, and that as grotesque a fate might come to be their own. Another bottle was broached to drink to a pleasant voyage, and the Governor would drink just one other on the top of it, so that the seamen were glad at last to stagger off—the one to his watch and the other to his bunk. But when after his four hours' spell the mate came down again, he was amazed to see the Governor in his Ramillies wig, his glasses, and his powdering-gown still seated sedately at the lonely table with his reeking pipe and six black bottles by his side.

"I have drunk with the Governor of St. Kitt's when he was sick," said he, "and God forbid that I should ever try to keep pace with him when he is well."

The voyage of the *Morning Star* was a successful one, and in about three weeks she was at the mouth of the British Channel. From the first day the infirm Governor had begun to recover his strength, and before they were halfway across the Atlantic he was, save only for his eyes, as well as any man upon the ship. Those who uphold the nourishing qualities of wine might point to him in triumph, for never a night passed that he did not repeat the performance of his first one. And yet he would be out upon deck in the early morning as fresh and brisk as the best of them, peering about with his weak eyes, and asking questions about the sails and the rigging, for he was anxious to learn the ways of the sea. And he made up for the deficiency of his eyes by obtaining leave from the captain that the New England seaman—he who had been cast away in the boat—should lead him about, and above all that he should sit beside him when he played cards and count the number of the pips, for unaided he could not tell the king from the knave.

It was natural that this Evanson should do the Governor willing service, since the one was the victim of the vile Sharkey, and the other was his avenger. One could see that it was a pleasure to the big American to lend his arm to the invalid, and at night he would stand with all respect behind his chair in the cabin and lay his great stub-nailed forefinger upon the card which he should play. Between them there was little in the pockets either of Captain Scarrow or of Morgan, the first mate, by the time they sighted the Lizard.

And it was not long before they found that all they had heard of the high temper of Sir Charles Ewan fell short of the mark. At a sign of opposition or a word or argument his chin would shoot out from his cravat, his masterful nose would be cocked at a higher and more insolent angle, and his bamboo cane would whistle up over his shoulder. He cracked it once over the head of the carpenter when the man had accidentally jostled him upon the deck. Once, too, when there was some grumbling and talk of a mutiny over the state of the provisions, he was of opinion that they should not wait for the dogs to rise, but that they should march forward and set upon them until they had trounced the devilment out of them. "Give me a knife and a bucket!" he cried with an oath, and could hardly be withheld from setting forth alone to deal with the spokesman of the seamen.

Captain Scarrow had to remind him that though he might be only answerable to himself at St. Kitt's, killing became murder upon the high seas. In politics he was, as became his official position, a stout prop of the House of Hanover, and he swore in his cups that he had never met a Jacobite without pistolling him where he stood. Yet for all his vaporing and his violence he was so good a companion, with such a stream of strange anecdote and reminiscence, that Scarrow and Morgan had never known a voyage pass so pleasantly.

And then at length came the last day, when, after passing the island, they had struck land again at the high white cliffs at Beachy Head. As evening fell, the ship lay rolling in an oily calm, a league off from Winchelsea, with the long dark snout of Dungeness jutting out in front of her. Next morning they would pick up their pilot at the Foreland, and Sir Charles might meet the king's ministers at Westminster before the evening. The boatswain had the watch, and the three friends were met for a last turn of cards in the cabin, the faithful American still serving as eyes to the Governor. There was a good stake upon the table, for the sailors had tried on this last night to win their losses back from their passenger. Suddenly he threw his cards down.

"The game's mine!" said he.

"Heh, Sir Charles, not so fast!" cried Captain Scarrow. "You have not played out the hand, and we are not the losers."

"Sink you for a liar!" said the Governor. "I tell you that I *have* played out the hand, and that you *are* a loser." He whipped off his wig and his glasses as he spoke, and there was a high, bald forehead, and a pair of shifty blue eyes with the red rims of a bull terrier.

"Good God!" cried the mate. "It's Sharkey!"

The two sailors sprang from their seats, but the big American castaway had put his huge back against the cabin door, and he held a pistol in each of his hands. The passenger had also laid a pistol upon the scattered cards in front of him. He burst into his high, neighing laugh as he swept all the money into the pocket of his silken green waistcoat.

"Captain Sharkey is the name, gentlemen," said he, "and this is Roaring

Ned Galloway, the quartermaster of the *Happy Delivery*. We made it hot, and so they marooned us: me on a dry Tortuga cay, and him in an oarless boat. You dogs—you poor, fond, water-hearted dogs—we hold you at the end of our pistols!"

"You may shoot, or you may not!" cried Scarrow, striking his hand upon the breast of his frieze jacket. "If it's my last breath, Sharkey, I tell you that you are a bloody rogue and miscreant, with a halter and hell fire in store for you!"

"There's a man of spirit, and one of my own kidney, and he's going to make a very pretty death of it!" cried Sharkey. "There's no one aft save the man at the wheel, so you may keep your breath, for you'll need it soon. Is the dinghy astern, Ned?"

"Ay, ay, captain!"

"And the other boats scuttled?"

"I bored them all in three places."

"Then we shall have to leave you, Captain Scarrow. You look as if you hadn't quite got your bearings yet. Is there anything you'd like to ask me?"

"I believe you're the devil himself!" cried the captain. "Where is the Governor of St. Kitt's?"

"When last I saw him, his Excellency was in bed with his throat cut. When I broke prison, I learnt from my friends—for Captain Sharkey has those who love him in every port—that the Governor was starting for Europe under a master who had never seen him. I climbed his verandah and I paid him the little debt that I owed him. Then I came aboard you with such of his things as I had need of, and a pair of glasses to hide these telltale eyes of mine, and I have ruffled it as a governor should. Now, Ned, you can get to work upon them."

"Help! Help! Watch ahoy!" yelled the mate; but the butt of the pirate's pistol crashed down on to his head, and he dropped like a pithed ox.

Scarrow rushed for the door, but the sentinel clapped his hand over his mouth, and threw his other arm round his waist.

"No use, Master Scarrow," said Sharkey. "Let us see you go down on your knees and beg for your life."

"I'll see you—" cried Scarrow, shaking his mouth clear.

"Twist his arm round, Ned. Now will you?"

"No; not if you twist it off."

"Put an inch of your knife into him."

"You may put six inches, and then I won't."

"Sink me, but I like his spirit!" cried Sharkey. "Put your knife in your pocket, Ned. You've saved your skin, Scarrow, and it's a pity so stout a man should not take to the only trade where a pretty fellow can pick up a living. You must be born for no common death, Scarrow, since you have lain at my mercy and lived to tell the story. Tie him up, Ned."

"To the stove, captain?"

"Tut, tut! there's a fire in the stove. None of your rover tricks, Ned Galloway, unless they are called for, or I'll let you know which of us two is captain and which is quartermaster. Make him fast to the table."

"Nay, I thought you meant to roast him!" said the quartermaster. "You surely do not mean to let him go?"

"If you and I were marooned on a Bahama cay, Ned Galloway, it is still for me to command and for you to obey. Sink you for a villain, do you dare to question my orders?"

"Nay, nay, Captain Sharkey, not so hot, sir!" said the quartermaster, and, lifting Scarrow like a child, he laid him on the table. With the quick dexterity of a seaman, he tied his spread-eagled hands and feet with a rope which was passed underneath, and gagged him securely with the long cravat which used to adorn the chin of the Governor of St. Kitt's.

"Now, Captain Scarrow, we must take our leave of you," said the pirate.

"If I had half a dozen of my brisk boys at my heels, I should have had your cargo and your ship, but Roaring Ned could not find a foremast hand with the spirit of a mouse. I see there are some small craft about, and we shall get one of them. When Captain Sharkey has a boat he can get a smack, when he has a smack he can get a brig, when he has a brig he can get a barque, and when he has a barque he'll soon have a full-rigged ship of his own—so make haste into London town, or I may be coming back, after all, for the *Morning Star*."

Captain Scarrow heard the key turn in the lock as they left the cabin. Then, as he strained at his bonds, he heard their footsteps pass up the companion and along the quarterdeck to where the dinghy hung in the stern. Then, still struggling and writhing, he heard the creak of the falls and the splash of the boat in the water. In a mad fury he tore and dragged at his ropes, until at last, with flayed wrists and ankles, he rolled from the table, sprang over the dead mate, kicked his way through the closed door, and rushed hatless on to the deck.

"Ahoy! Peterson, Armitage, Wilson!" he screamed. "Cutlasses and pistols! Clear away the longboat! Clear away the gig! Sharkey, the pirate, is in yonder dinghy. Whistle up the larboard watch, bo'sun, and tumble into the boats all hands."

Down splashed the longboat and down splashed the gig, but in an instant the coxswains and crews were swarming up on to the deck once more.

"The boats are scuttled!" they cried. "They are leaking like a sieve."

The captain remembered Sharkey's taunt. He gave a bitter curse. He had been beaten and outwitted at every point. Above was a cloudless, starlit sky, with neither wind nor the promise of it. The sails flapped idly in the moonlight. Far away lay a fishing smack, with the men clustering over their net.

Close to them was the little dinghy, dipping and lifting over the shining swell.

"They are dead men!" cried the captain. "A shout all together, boys, to warn them of their danger."

But it was too late.

At that very moment the dinghy shot into the shadow of the fishing boat. There were two rapid pistol shots, a scream, and then another pistol shot, followed by silence. The clustering fishermen had disappeared. And then, suddenly, as the first puffs of a land breeze came out from the Sussex shore, the boom swung out, the mainsail filled, and the little craft crept out with her nose to the Atlantic.

"The Island Come True"
from *Peter Pan*

J. M. Barrie

Feeling that Peter was on his way back, the Neverland had again woke into life. We ought to use the pluperfect and say wakened, but woke is better and was always used by Peter.

In his absence things are usually quiet on the island. The fairies take an hour longer in the morning, the beasts attend to their young, the Indians feast for six days and nights, and when pirates and lost boys meet they merely bite their thumbs at each other. But with the coming of Peter, who hates lethargy, they are all under way again: if you put your ear to the ground now, you would hear the whole island seething with life.

On this evening the chief forces of the island were disposed as follows. The lost boys were out looking for Peter, the pirates were out looking for the lost boys, the Indians were out looking for the pirates, and the beasts were out looking for the Indians. They were going round and round the island, but they did not meet because all were going at the same rate.

All wanted blood except the boys, who liked it as a rule, but tonight were out to greet their captain. The boys on the island vary, of course, in numbers, according as they get killed and so on; and when they seem to be growing up, which is against the rules, Peter thins them out; but at this time there were six of them, counting the Twins as two. Let us pretend to lie here among the sugarcane and watch them as they steal by in single file, each with his hand on his dagger.

They are forbidden by Peter to look in the least like him, and they wear the skins of bears slain by themselves, in which they are so round and furry that when they fall they roll. They have therefore become very surefooted.

The first to pass is Tootles, not the least brave but the most unfortunate of all that gallant band. He had been in fewer adventures than any of them, because the big things constantly happened just when he had stepped round the corner; all would be quiet, he would take the opportunity of going off to gather a few sticks for firewood, and then when he returned the others would be sweeping up the blood. The ill luck had given a gentle melancholy to his countenance, but instead of souring his nature had sweetened it, so that he was quite the humblest of the boys. Poor kind Tootles, there is danger in the air for you tonight. Take care lest an adventure is now offered you, which, if accepted, will plunge you in deepest woe. Tootles, the fairy Tink, who is bent on mischief this night, is looking for a tool, and she thinks you the most easily tricked of the boys. 'Ware Tinker Bell.

Would that he could hear us, but we are not really on the island, and he passes by, biting his knuckles.

Next comes Nibs, the gay and debonair, followed by Slightly, who cuts whistles out of the trees and dances ecstatically to his own tunes. Slightly is the most conceited of the boys. He thinks he remembers the days before he was lost, with their manners and customs, and this has given his nose an offensive tilt. Curly is fourth; he is a pickle, and so often has he had to deliver up his person when Peter said sternly, "Stand forth the one who did this thing," that now at the command he stands forth automatically whether he has done it or not. Last come the Twins, who cannot be described because we should be sure to be describing the wrong one. Peter never quite knew what twins were, and his band were not allowed to know anything he did not know, so these two were always vague about themselves, and did their best to give satisfaction by keeping close together in an apologetic sort of way.

The boys vanish in the gloom, and after a pause, but not a long pause, for things go briskly on the island, come the pirates on their track. We hear them before they are seen, and it is always the same dreadful song:

"Avast belay, yo ho, heave to,
A-pirating we go,
And if we're parted by a shot
We're sure to meet below!"

A more villainous-looking lot never hung in a row on Execution dock. Here, a little in advance, ever and again with his head to the ground listening, his great arms bare, pieces of eight in his ears as ornaments, is the handsome Italian Cecco, who cut his name in letters of blood on the back of the governor of the prison at Goa. That gigantic African behind him has had many names since he dropped the one with which mothers still terrify their children on the banks of the Guidjo-mo. Here is Bill Jukes, every inch of him tattooed; and Cookson, said to be Black Murphy's brother (but this was never proved); and Gentleman Starkey, once an usher in a public school and still dainty in his ways of killing; and Skylights (Morgan's Skylights); and the Irish bo'sun Smee, an oddly genial man who stabbed, so to speak, without offense, and was the only Nonconformist in Hook's crew; and Noodler, whose hands were fixed on backwards; and Robt. Mullins and Alf Mason and many another ruffian long known and feared on the Spanish Main.

In the midst of them, the blackest and largest jewel in that dark setting, reclined James Hook, or, as he wrote himself, Jas. Hook, of whom it is said he was the only man that the Sea-Cook feared. He lay at his ease in a rough chariot drawn and propelled by his men, and instead of a right hand he had the iron hook with which ever and anon he encouraged them to increase their pace. As dogs this terrible man treated and addressed them, and as dogs they obeyed him. In person he was cadaverous and blackavised, and his hair was dressed in long curls, which at a little distance looked like black candles, and gave a singularly threatening expression to his handsome countenance. His eyes were of the blue of the forget-me-not, and of a profound melancholy, save when he was plunging his hook into you, at which time two red spots appeared in them and lit them up horribly. In manner, something of the grand seigneur still clung to him, so that he even ripped you up with an air, and I have been told that he was a *raconteur* of repute. He was never more sinister than when he was most polite, which is probably the truest test of breeding; and the elegance of his diction, even when he was swearing, no less than the distinction of his demeanor, showed him one of a different caste from his crew. A man of indomitable courage, it was said of him that the only thing he shied at was the sight of his own blood, which was thick and of an unusual color. In dress he somewhat aped the attire associated with the name of Charles II, having heard it said in some earlier period of his career that he bore a strange resemblance to the ill-fated Stuarts; and in his mouth he had a holder of his own contrivance which enabled him to smoke two cigars at once. But undoubtedly the grimmest part of him was his iron claw.

Let us now kill a pirate, to show Hook's method. Skylights will do. As they pass, Skylights lurches clumsily against him, ruffling his lace collar; the hook shoots forth, there is a tearing sound and one screech, then the body is kicked aside, and the pirates pass on. He has not even taken the cigars from his mouth.

Such is the terrible man against whom Peter Pan is pitted. Which will win?

On the trail of the pirates, stealing noiselessly down the warpath, which is not visible to inexperienced eyes, come the Indians, every one of them with his eyes peeled. They carry tomahawks and knives, and their bodies gleam with paint and oil. Strung around them are scalps, of boys as well as of pirates, for these are a fearsome tribe, and not to be confused with the softer-hearted Delawares or the Hurons. In the van, on all fours, is Great Big Little Panther, a warrior of so many scalps that in his present position they

somewhat impede his progress. Bringing up the rear, the place of greatest danger, comes beautiful Tiger Lily, proudly erect, a princess in her own right. There is not a warrior who would not have her to wife, but she staves off the altar with a hatchet. Observe how they pass over fallen twigs without making the slightest noise. The only sound to be heard is their somewhat heavy breathing. The fact is that they are all a little fat just now after the heavy gorging, but in time they will work this off. For the moment, however, it constitutes their chief danger.

The Indians disappear as they have come, like shadows, and soon their place is taken by the beasts, a great and motley procession: lions, tigers, bears, and the innumerable smaller savage things that flee from them, for every kind of beast, and, more particularly, all the man-eaters, live cheek by jowl on the favored island. Their tongues are hanging out; they are hungry tonight.

When they have passed, comes the last figure of all, a gigantic crocodile. We shall see for whom she is looking presently.

The crocodile passes, but soon the boys appear again, for the procession must continue indefinitely until one of the parties stops or changes its pace. Then quickly they will be on top of each other.

All are keeping a sharp lookout in front, but none suspects that the danger may be creeping up from behind. This shows how real the island was.

The first to fall out of the moving circle was the boys. They flung themselves down on the sward, close to their underground home.

"I do wish Peter would come back," every one of them said nervously, though in height and still more in breadth they were all larger than their captain.

"I am the only one who is not afraid of the pirates," Slightly said in the tone that prevented his being a general favorite; but perhaps some distant sound disturbed him, for he added hastily, "but I wish he would come back and tell us whether he has heard anything more about Cinderella."

They talked of Cinderella, and Tootles was confident that his mother must have been very like her.

It was only in Peter's absence that they could speak of mothers, the subject being forbidden by him as silly.

"All I remember about my mother," Nibs told them, "is that she often said to Father, 'Oh, how I wish I had a checkbook of my own.' I don't know what a checkbook is, but I should just love to give my mother one."

While they talked, they heard a distant sound. You or I, not being wild things of the woods, would have heard nothing, but they heard it, and it was the grim song:

"Yo ho, yo ho, the pirate life,
The flag o' skull and bones,
A merry hour, a hempen rope,
And hey for Davy Jones."

At once the lost boys—but where are they? They are no longer there. Rabbits could not have disappeared more quickly.

I will tell you where they are. With the exception of Nibs, who has darted away to reconnoiter, they are already in their home under the ground, a very delightful residence of which we shall see a good deal presently. But how have they reached it? For there is no entrance to be seen, not so much as a pile of brushwood which, if removed, would disclose the mouth of a cave. Look closely, however, and you may note that there are here seven large trees, each having in its hollow trunk a hole as large as a boy. These are the seven entrances to the home under the ground, for which Hook has been searching in vain these many moons. Will he find it tonight?

As the pirates advanced, the quick eye of Starkey sighted Nibs disappearing through the wood, and at once his pistol flashed out. But an iron claw gripped his shoulder.

"Captain, let go," he cried, writhing.

Now for the first time we hear the voice of Hook. It was a black voice. "Put back that pistol first," it said threateningly.

"It was one of those boys you hate. I could have shot him dead."

"Aye, and the sound would have brought Tiger Lily's Indians upon us. Do you want to lose your scalp?"

"Shall I after him, captain," asked pathetic Smee, "and tickle him with Johnny Corkscrew?" Smee had pleasant names for everything, and his cutlass was Johnny Corkscrew, because he wriggled it in the wound. One could mention many lovable traits in Smee. For instance, after killing, it was his spectacles he wiped instead of his weapon.

"Johnny's a silent fellow," he reminded Hook.

"Not now, Smee," Hook said darkly. "He is only one, and I want to mischief all the seven. Scatter and look for them."

The pirates disappeared among the trees, and in a moment their captain and Smee were alone. Hook heaved a heavy sigh; and I know not why it was, perhaps it was because of the soft beauty of the evening, but there came over him a desire to confide to his faithful bo'sun the story of his life. He spoke long and earnestly, but what it was all about Smee, who was rather stupid, did not know in the least.

Anon he caught the word Peter.

"Most of all," Hook was saying passionately, "I want their captain, Peter Pan. 'Twas he cut off my arm." He brandished the hook threateningly. "I've waited long to shake his hand with this. Oh, I'll tear him."

"And yet," said Smee, "I have often heard you say that hook was worth a score of hands, for combing the hair and other homely uses."

"Aye," the captain answered, "if I was a mother, I would pray to have my children born with this instead of that," and he cast a look of pride upon his iron hand and one of scorn upon the other. Then again he frowned.

"Peter flung my arm," he said, wincing, "to a crocodile that happened to be passing by."

"I have often," said Smee, "noticed your strange dread of crocodiles."

"Not of crocodiles," Hook corrected him, "but of that one crocodile." He lowered his voice. "It liked my arm so much, Smee, that it has followed me ever since, from sea to sea and from land to land, licking its lips for the rest of me."

"In a way," said Smee, "it's a sort of compliment."

"I want no such compliments," Hook barked petulantly. "I want Peter Pan, who first gave the brute its taste for me."

He sat down on a large mushroom, and now there was a quiver in his voice. "Smee," he said huskily, "that crocodile would have had me before this, but by a lucky chance it swallowed a clock which goes tick tick inside it, and so before it can reach me I hear the tick and bolt." He laughed, but in a hollow way.

"Some day," said Smee, "the clock will run down, and then he'll get you."

Hook wetted his dry lips. "Aye," he said, "that's the fear that haunts me."

Since sitting down, he had felt curiously warm. "Smee," he said, "this seat is hot." He jumped up. "Odds bobs, hammer and tongs, I'm burning."

They examined the mushroom, which was of a size and solidity unknown on the mainland; they tried to pull it up, and it came away at once in their hands, for it had no root. Stranger still, smoke began at once to ascend. The pirates looked at each other. "A chimney!" they both exclaimed.

They had indeed discovered the chimney of the home under the ground.

It was the custom of the boys to stop it with a mushroom when enemies were in the neighborhood.

Not only smoke came out of it. There came also children's voices, for so safe did the boys feel in their hiding place that they were gaily chattering. The pirates listened grimly, and then replaced the mushroom. They looked around them and noted the holes in the seven trees.

"Did you hear them say Peter Pan's from home?" Smee whispered, fidgeting with Johnny Corkscrew.

Hook nodded. He stood for a long time lost in thought, and at last a curdling smile lit up his swarthy face. Smee had been waiting for it. "Unrip your plan, captain," he cried eagerly.

"To return to the ship," Hook replied slowly through his teeth, "and cook a large rich cake of a jolly thickness with green sugar on it. There can be but one room below, for there is but one chimney. The silly moles had not the sense to see that they did not need a door apiece. That shows they have no mother. We will leave the cake on the shore of the mermaids' lagoon. These boys are always swimming about there, playing with the mermaids. They will find the cake and they will gobble it up, because, having no mother, they don't know how dangerous 'tis to eat rich damp cake." He burst into laughter, not hollow laughter now, but honest laughter. "Aha, they will die."

Smee had listened with growing admiration.

"It's the wickedest, prettiest policy ever I heard of," he cried, and in their exultation they danced and sang:

"Avast, belay, when I appear,
By fear they're overtook;
Naught's left upon your bones when you
Have shaken claws with Hook."

They began the verse, but they never finished it, for another sound broke in and stilled them. It was at first such a tiny sound that a leaf might have fallen on it and smothered it, but as it came nearer it was more distinct.

Tick tick tick tick.

Hook stood shuddering, one foot in the air.

"The crocodile," he gasped, and bounded away, followed by his bo'sun.

It was indeed the crocodile. It had passed the Indians, who were now on the trail of the other pirates. It oozed on after Hook.

Once more the boys emerged into the open; but the dangers of the night were not yet over, for presently Nibs rushed breathless into their midst, pursued by a pack of wolves. The tongues of the pursuers were hanging out; the baying of them was horrible.

"Save me, save me!" cried Nibs, falling on the ground.

"But what can we do, what can we do?"

It was a high compliment to Peter that at that dire moment their thoughts turned to him.

"What would Peter do?" they cried simultaneously.

Almost in the same breath they added, "Peter would look at them through his legs."

And then, "Let us do what Peter would do."

It is quite the most successful way of defying wolves, and as one boy they bent and looked through their legs.

The next moment is the long one; but victory came quickly, for as the boys advanced upon them in this terrible attitude, the wolves dropped their tails and fled.

Now Nibs rose from the ground, and the others thought that his staring eyes still saw the wolves. But it was not wolves he saw.

"I have seen a wonderfuller thing," he cried as they gathered round him eagerly. "A great white bird. It is flying this way."

"What kind of a bird, do you think?"

"I don't know," Nibs said, awestruck, "but it looks so weary, and as it flies it moans, 'Poor Wendy.'"

"Poor Wendy?"

"I remember," said Slightly instantly, "there are birds called Wendies."

"See, it comes," cried Curly, pointing to Wendy in the heavens.

Wendy was now almost overhead, and they could hear her plaintive cry. But more distinct came the shrill voice of Tinker Bell. The jealous fairy had now cast off all disguise of friendship, and was darting at her victim from every direction, pinching savagely each time she touched.

"Hallo, Tink," cried the wondering boys.

Tink's reply rang out: "Peter wants you to shoot the Wendy."

It was not in their nature to question when Peter ordered. "Let us do what Peter wishes," cried the simple boys. "Quick, bows and arrows."

All but Tootles popped down their trees. He had a bow and arrow with him, and Tink noted it, and rubbed her little hands.

"Quick, Tootles, quick," she screamed. "Peter will be so pleased."

Tootles excitedly fitted the arrow to his bow. "Out of the way, Tink," he shouted; and then he fired, and Wendy fluttered to the ground with an arrow in her breast.

"The Rebels-Convict" from *Captain Blood*

Rafael Sabatini

There were, when the purple gloom of the tropical night descended upon the Caribbean, not more than ten men on guard aboard the *Cinco Llagas*, so confident—and with good reason—were the Spaniards of the complete subjection of the islanders. And when I say that there were ten men on guard, I state rather the purpose for which they were left aboard than the duty which they fulfilled. As a matter of fact, whilst the main body of the Spaniards feasted and rioted ashore, the Spanish gunner and his crew—who had so nobly done their duty and ensured the easy victory of the day—were feasting on the gun-deck upon the wine and the fresh meats fetched out to them from shore. Above, two sentinels only kept vigil, at stem and stern. Nor were they as vigilant as they should have been, or else they must have observed the two wherries that under cover of the darkness came gliding from the wharf, with well-greased rowlocks, to bring up in silence under the great ship's quarter.

From the gallery aft still hung the ladder by which Don Diego had descended to the boat that had taken him ashore. The sentry on guard in the stern, coming presently round this gallery, was suddenly confronted by the black shadow of a man standing before him at the head of the ladder.

"Who's there?" he asked, but without alarm, supposing it one of his fellows.

"It is I," softly answered Peter Blood in the fluent Castilian of which he was master.

"Is it you, Pedro?" The Spaniard came a step nearer.

"Peter is my name; but I doubt I'll not be the Peter you're expecting."

"How?" quoth the sentry, checking.

"This way," said Mr. Blood.

The wooden taffrail was a low one, and the Spaniard was taken completely by surprise. Save for the splash he made as he struck the water, narrowly missing a boat that waited under the counter, not a sound announced his misadventure. Armed as he was with corselet, cuissarts, and headpiece, he sank to trouble them no more.

"Whist!" hissed Mr. Blood to his waiting rebels-convict. "Come on, now, and without noise."

Within five minutes they had swarmed aboard, the entire twenty of them overflowing from that narrow gallery and crouching on the quarterdeck itself. Lights showed ahead. Under the great lantern in the prow they saw the black figure of the other sentry, pacing on the forecastle. From below sounds reached them of the orgy on the gun-deck: a rich male voice was singing an obscene ballad to which the others chanted in chorus:

"Y estos son los usos de Castilla y de Leon!"

"From what I've seen today I can well believe it," said Mr. Blood, and whispered: "Forward—after me."

Crouching low, they glided, noiseless as shadows, to the quarterdeck rail, and thence slipped without sound down into the waist. Two-thirds of them were armed with muskets, some of which they had found in the overseer's house, and others supplied from the secret hoard that Mr. Blood had so laboriously assembled against the day of escape. The remainder were equipped with knives and cutlasses.

In the vessel's waist they hung awhile, until Mr. Blood had satisfied himself that no other sentinel showed above decks but that inconvenient fellow in the prow. Their first attention must be for him. Mr. Blood, himself, crept forward with two companions, leaving the others in the charge of that Nathaniel Hagthorpe whose sometime commission in the King's Navy gave him the best title to this office.

Mr. Blood's absence was brief. When he rejoined his comrades, there was no watch above the Spaniards' decks.

Meanwhile the revelers below continued to make merry at their ease in the conviction of complete security. The garrison of Barbados was overpowered and disarmed, and their companions were ashore in complete possession of the town, glutting themselves hideously upon the fruits of victory. What, then, was there to fear? Even when their quarters were invaded and they found themselves surrounded by a score of wild, hairy, half-naked men, who—save that they appeared once to have been white—looked like a horde of savages, the Spaniards could not believe their eyes.

Who could have dreamed that a handful of forgotten plantation-slaves would have dared to take so much upon themselves?

The half-drunken Spaniards, their laughter suddenly quenched, the song perishing on their lips, stared, stricken and bewildered, at the leveled muskets by which they were checkmated.

And then, from out of this uncouth pack of savages that beset them, stepped a slim, tall fellow with light-blue eyes in a tawny face, eyes in which glinted the light of a wicked humor. He addressed them in the purest Castilian.

"You will save yourselves pain and trouble by regarding yourselves my prisoners, and suffering yourselves to be quietly bestowed out of harm's way."

"Name of God!" swore the gunner, which did no justice at all to an amazement beyond expression.

"If you please," said Mr. Blood, and thereupon those gentlemen of Spain were induced without further trouble beyond a musket prod or two to drop through a scuttle to the deck below.

After that the rebels-convict refreshed themselves with the good things in the consumption of which they had interrupted the Spaniards. To taste palatable Christian food after months of salt fish and maize dumplings was in itself a feast to these unfortunates. But there were no excesses. Mr. Blood saw to that, although it required all the firmness of which he was capable.

Dispositions were to be made without delay against that which must follow before they could abandon themselves fully to the enjoyment of their victory. This, after all, was no more than a preliminary skirmish, although it was one that afforded them the key to the situation. It remained to dispose so that the utmost profit might be drawn from it. Those dispositions occupied some very considerable portion of the night. But, at least, they were complete before the sun peeped over the shoulder of Mount Hillbay to shed his light upon a day of some surprises.

It was soon after sunrise that the rebel-convict who paced the quarter-deck in Spanish corselet and headpiece, a Spanish musket on his shoulder, announced the approach of a boat. It was Don Diego de Espinosa y Valdez coming aboard with four great treasure chests, containing each twenty-five thousand pieces of eight, the ransom delivered to him at dawn by Governor Steed. He was accompanied by his son, Don Esteban, and by six men who took the oars.

Aboard the frigate all was quiet and orderly as it should be. She rode at anchor, her larboard to the shore, and the main ladder on her starboard side. Round to this came the boat with Don Diego and his treasure. Mr. Blood had disposed effectively. It was not for nothing that he had served under de Ruyter. The swings were waiting, and the windlass manned. Below, a gun-crew held itself in readiness under the command of Ogle, who had been a gunner in the Royal Navy before he went in for politics and followed the fortunes of the Duke of Monmouth. He was a sturdy, resolute fellow who inspired confidence by the very confidence he displayed in himself.

Don Diego mounted the ladder and stepped upon the deck, alone, and entirely unsuspicious. What should the poor man suspect?

Before he could even look round, and survey this guard drawn up to receive him, a tap over the head with a capstan bar efficiently handled by Hagthorpe put him to sleep without the least fuss.

He was carried away to his cabin, whilst the treasure chests, handled by the men he had left in the boat, were being hauled to the deck. That being satisfactorily accomplished, Don Esteban and the fellows who had manned the boat came up the ladder, one by one, to be handled with the same quiet efficiency. Peter Blood had a genius for these things, and almost, I suspect, an eye for the dramatic. Dramatic, certainly, was the spectacle now offered to the survivors of the raid.

With Colonel Bishop at their head, and gout-ridden Governor Steed sitting on the ruins of a wall beside him, they glumly watched the departure of the eight boats containing the weary Spanish ruffians who had glutted themselves with rapine, murder, and violences unspeakable.

They looked on, between relief at this departure of their remorseless enemies, and despair at the wild ravages which, temporarily at least, had wrecked the prosperity and happiness of that little colony.

The boats pulled away from the shore, with their loads of laughing, jeering Spaniards, who were still flinging taunts across the water at their surviving victims. They had come midway between the wharf and the ship, when suddenly the air was shaken by the boom of a gun.

A round shot struck the water within a fathom of the foremost boat, sending a shower of spray over its occupants. They paused at their oars, astounded into silence for a moment. Then speech burst from them like an explosion. Angrily voluble, they anathematized this dangerous carelessness on the part of their gunner, who should know better than to fire a salute from a cannon loaded with shot. They were still cursing him when a second shot, better aimed than the first, came to crumple one of the boats into splinters, flinging its crew, dead and living, into the water.

But if it silenced these, it gave tongue, still more angry, vehement, and bewildered to the crews of the other seven boats. From each the suspended oars stood out poised over the water, whilst on their feet in the excitement the Spaniards screamed oaths at the ship, begging Heaven and Hell to inform them what madman had been let loose among her guns.

Plump into their middle came a third shot, smashing a second boat with fearful execution. Followed again a moment of awful silence, then among those Spanish pirates all was gibbering and jabbering and splashing of oars, as they attempted to pull in every direction at once. Some were for going ashore, others for heading straight to the vessel and there discovering what might be amiss. That something was very gravely amiss there could be no further doubt, particularly as whilst they discussed and fumed and cursed two more shots came over the water to account for yet a third of their boats.

The resolute Ogle was making excellent practice, and fully justifying his claims to know something of gunnery. In their consternation the Spaniards had simplified his task by huddling their boats together.

After the fourth shot, opinion was no longer divided amongst them. As with one accord they went about, or attempted to do so, for before they had

accomplished it two more of their boats had been sunk.

The three boats that remained, without concerning themselves with their more unfortunate fellows, who were struggling in the water, headed back for the wharf at speed.

If the Spaniards understood nothing of all this, the forlorn islanders ashore understood still less, until to help their wits they saw the flag of Spain come down from the mainmast of the *Cinco Llagas*, and the flag of England soar to its empty place. Even then some bewilderment persisted, and it was with fearful eyes that they observed the return of their enemies, who might vent upon them the ferocity aroused by these extraordinary events.

Ogle, however, continued to give proof that his knowledge of gunnery was not of yesterday. After the fleeing Spaniards went his shots. The last of their boats flew into splinters as it touched the wharf, and its remains were buried under a shower of loosened masonry.

That was the end of this pirate crew, which not ten minutes ago had been laughingly counting up the pieces of eight that would fall to the portion of each for his share in that act of villainy. Close upon threescore survivors contrived to reach the shore. Whether they had cause for congratulation, I am unable to say in the absence of any records in which their fate may be traced. That lack of records is in itself eloquent. We know that they were made fast as they landed, and considering the offense they had given I am not disposed to doubt that they had every reason to regret the survival.

The mystery of the succor that had come at the eleventh hour to wreak vengeance upon the Spaniards, and to preserve for the island the extortionate ransom of a hundred thousand pieces of eight, remained yet to be probed. That the *Cinco Llagas* was now in friendly hands could no longer be doubted after the proofs it had given. But who, the people of Bridgetown asked one another, were the men in possession of her, and whence had they come? The only possible assumption ran the truth very closely. A resolute party of islanders must have got aboard during the night, and seized the ship. It remained to ascertain the precise identity of these mysterious saviors, and do them fitting honor.

Upon this errand—Governor Steed's condition not permitting him to go in person—went Colonel Bishop as the Governor's deputy, attended by two officers.

As he stepped from the ladder into the vessel's waist, the Colonel beheld there, beside the main hatch, the four treasure chests, the contents of one of which had been contributed almost entirely by himself. It was a gladsome spectacle, and his eyes sparkled in beholding it.

Ranged on either side, athwart the deck, stood a score of men in two well-ordered files, with breasts and backs of steel, polished Spanish morions on their heads, overshadowing their faces, and muskets ordered at their sides.

Colonel Bishop could not be expected to recognize at a glance in these upright, furbished, soldierly figures the ragged, unkempt scarecrows that but yesterday had been toiling in his plantations. Still less could he be expected to recognize at once the courtly gentleman who advanced to greet him—a lean, graceful gentleman, dressed in the Spanish fashion, all in black with silver lace, a gold-hilted sword dangling beside him from a gold embroidered baldrick, a broad castor with a sweeping plume set above carefully curled ringlets of deepest black.

"Be welcome aboard the *Cinco Llagas*, Colonel, darling," a voice vaguely familiar addressed the planter. "We've made the best of the Spaniards' wardrobe in honor of this visit, though it was scarcely yourself we had dared hope to expect. You find yourself among friends—old friends of yours, all."

The Colonel stared in stupefaction. Mr. Blood tricked out in all this splendor—indulging therein his natural taste—his face carefully shaven, his hair as carefully dressed, seemed transformed into a younger man. The fact is he looked no more than the thirty-three years he counted to his age.

"Peter Blood!" It was an ejaculation of amazement. Satisfaction followed

swiftly. "Was it you, then . . . ?"

"Myself it was—myself and these, my good friends and yours." Mr. Blood tossed back the fine lace from his wrist, to wave a hand towards the file of men standing to attention there.

The Colonel looked more closely. "Gad's my life!" he crowed on a note of foolish jubilation. "And it was with these fellows that you took the Spaniard and turned the tables on those dogs! Oddswounds! It was heroic!"

"Heroic, is it? Bedad, it's epic! Ye begin to perceive the breadth and depth of my genius."

Colonel Bishop sat himself down on the hatch-coaming, took off his broad hat, and mopped his brow.

"Y' amaze me!" he gasped. "On my soul, y' amaze me! To have recovered the treasure and to have seized this fine ship and all she'll hold! It will be something to set against the other losses we have suffered. As Gad's my life, you deserve well for this."

"I am entirely of your opinion."

"Damme! You all deserve well, and damme, you shall find me grateful."

"That's as it should be," said Mr. Blood. "The question is how well we deserve, and how grateful shall we find you?"

Colonel Bishop considered him. There was a shadow of surprise in his face.

"Why—his excellency shall write home an account of your exploit, and maybe some portion of your sentences shall be remitted."

"The generosity of King James is well known," sneered Nathaniel Hagthorpe, who was standing by, and amongst the ranged rebels-convict someone ventured to laugh.

Colonel Bishop started up. He was pervaded by the first pang of uneasiness. It occurred to him that all here might not be as friendly as appeared.

"And there's another matter," Mr. Blood resumed. "There's a matter of a flogging that's due to me. Ye're a man of your word in such matters,

Colonel—if not perhaps in others—and ye said, I think, that ye'd not leave a square inch of skin on my back."

The planter waved the matter aside. Almost it seemed to offend him.

"Tush! Tush! After this splendid deed of yours, do you suppose I can be thinking of such things?"

"I'm glad ye feel like that about it. But I'm thinking it's mighty lucky for me the Spaniards didn't come today instead of yesterday, or it's in the same plight as Jeremy Pitt I'd be this minute. And in that case where was the genius that would have turned the tables on these rascally Spaniards?"

"Why speak of it now?"

"I must, Colonel, darling. Ye've worked a deal of wickedness and cruelty in your time, and I want this to be a lesson to you, a lesson that ye'll remember—for the sake of others who may come after us. There's Jeremy up there in the roundhouse with a back that's every color of the rainbow; and the poor lad'll not be himself again for a month. And if it hadn't been for the Spaniards, maybe it's dead he'd be by now, and maybe myself with him."

Hagthorpe lounged forward. He was a fairly tall, vigorous man with a clear-cut, attractive face which in itself announced his breeding.

"Why will you be wasting words on the hog?" wondered that sometime officer in the Royal Navy. "Fling him overboard and have done with him."

The Colonel's eyes bulged in his head. "What the devil do you mean?" he blustered.

"It's the lucky man ye are entirely, Colonel, though ye don't guess the source of your good fortune."

And now another intervened—the brawny, one-eyed Wolverstone, less mercifully disposed than his more gentlemanly fellow-convict.

"String him up from the yardarm," he cried, his deep voice harsh and angry, and more than one of the slaves standing to their arms made echo.

Colonel Bishop trembled. Mr. Blood turned. He was quite calm.

"If you please, Wolverstone," said he, "I conduct affairs in my own way. That is the pact. You'll please to remember it." His eyes looked along the ranks, making it plain that he addressed them all. "I desire that Colonel Bishop should have his life. One reason is that I require him as a hostage. If ye insist on hanging him, ye'll have to hang me with him, or in the alternative I'll go ashore."

He paused. There was no answer. But they stood hangdog and half-mutinous before him, save Hagthorpe, who shrugged and smiled wearily.

Mr. Blood resumed: "Ye'll please to understand that aboard a ship there is one captain. So." He swung again to the startled Colonel. "Though I promise you your life, I must—as you've heard—keep you aboard as a hostage for the good behavior of Governor Steed and what's left of the fort until we put to sea."

"Until you . . ." Horror prevented Colonel Bishop from echoing the remainder of that incredible speech.

"Just so," said Peter Blood, and he turned to the officers who had accompanied the Colonel. "The boat is waiting, gentlemen. You'll have heard what I said. Convey it with my compliments to his excellency."

"But, sir . . ." one of them began.

"There is no more to be said, gentlemen. My name is Blood—Captain Blood, if you please, of this ship the *Cinco Llagas*, taken as a prize of war from Don Diego de Espinosa y Valdez, who is my prisoner aboard. You are to understand that I have turned the tables on more than the Spaniards. There's the ladder. You'll find it more convenient than being heaved over the side, which is what'll happen if you linger."

They went, though not without some hustling, regardless of the bellowings of Colonel Bishop, whose monstrous rage was fanned by terror at finding himself at the mercy of these men of whose cause to hate him he was very fully conscious.

A half dozen of them, apart from Jeremy Pitt, who was utterly incapacitated for the present, possessed a superficial knowledge of seamanship. Hagthorpe, although he had been a fighting officer, untrained in navigation, knew how to handle a ship, and under his directions they set about getting under way.

The anchor catted, and the mainsail unfurled, they stood out for the open before a gentle breeze, without interference from the fort.

As they were running close to the headland east of the bay, Peter Blood returned to the Colonel, who, under guard and panic-stricken, had dejectedly resumed his seat on the coamings of the main hatch.

"Can ye swim, Colonel?"

Colonel Bishop looked up. His great face was yellow and seemed in that moment of a preternatural flabbiness; his beady eyes were beadier than ever.

"As your doctor, now, I prescribe a swim to cool the excessive heat of your humors." Blood delivered the explanation pleasantly, and, receiving still no answer from the Colonel, continued: "It's a mercy for you I'm not by nature as bloodthirsty as some of my friends here. And it's the devil's own labor I've had to prevail upon them not to be vindictive. I doubt if ye're worth the pains I've taken for you."

He was lying. He had no doubt at all. Had he followed his own wishes and instincts, he would certainly have strung the Colonel up and accounted it a meritorious deed. It was the thought of Arabella Bishop that had urged him to mercy and had led him to oppose the natural vindictiveness of his fellow-slaves until he had been in danger of precipitating a mutiny. It was entirely to the fact that the Colonel was her uncle, although he did not even begin to suspect such a cause, that he owed such mercy as was now being shown him.

"You shall have a chance to swim for it," Peter Blood continued. "It's not above a quarter of a mile to the headland yonder, and with ordinary luck ye should manage it. Faith, you're fat enough to float. Come on! Now, don't be hesitating or it's a long voyage ye'll be going with us, and the devil knows what may happen to you. You're not loved any more than you deserve."

Colonel Bishop mastered himself, and rose. A merciless despot, who had never known the need for restraint in all these years, he was doomed by ironic fate to practice restraint in the very moment when his feelings had reached their most violent intensity.

Peter Blood gave an order. A plank was run out over the gunwale, and lashed down.

"If you please, Colonel," said he, with a graceful flourish of invitation.

The Colonel looked at him, and there was hell in his glance. Then, taking his resolve, and putting the best face upon it, since no other could help him here, he peeled off his fine coat of biscuit-colored taffetas, and climbed upon the plank.

A moment he paused, steadied by a hand that clutched the ratlines, looking down in terror at the green water rushing past some five and twenty feet below.

"Just take a little walk, Colonel, darling," said a smooth, mocking voice behind him.

Still clinging, Colonel Bishop looked round in hesitation, and saw the bulwarks lined with swarthy faces—the faces of men that as lately as yesterday would have turned pale under his frown, faces that were now all wickedly agrin.

For a moment rage stamped out his fear. He cursed them aloud venomously and incoherently, then loosed his hold and stepped out upon the plank. Three steps he took before he lost his balance and went tumbling into the green depths below.

When he came to the surface again, gasping for air, the *Cinco Llagas* was already some furlongs to leeward. But the roaring cheer of mocking valediction from the rebels-convict reached him across the water, to drive the iron of impotent rage deeper into his soul.

"A Ballad of John Silver"

John Masefield

We were schooner-rigged and rakish, with a long and lissome hull,
And we flew the pretty colors of the crossbones and the skull;
We'd a big black Jolly Roger flapping grimly at the fore,
And we sailed the Spanish Water in the happy days of yore.

We'd a long brass gun amidships, like a well-conducted ship,
We had each a brace of pistols and a cutlass at the hip;
It's a point which tells against us, and a fact to be deplored,
But we chased the goodly merchantmen and laid their ships aboard.

Then the dead men fouled the scuppers and the wounded filled the chains,

90

And the paint-work all was spatter-dashed with other people's brains,
She was boarded, she was looted, she was scuttled till she sank,
And the pale survivors left us by the medium of the plank.

O! then it was (while standing by the taffrail on the poop)
We could hear the drowning folk lament the absent chicken-coop;
Then, having washed the blood away, we'd little else to do
Than to dance a quiet hornpipe as the old salts taught us to.

O! the fiddle on the fo'c's'le, and the slapping naked soles,
And the genial "Down the middle, Jake, and curtsy when she rolls!"
With the silver seas around us and the pale moon overhead,
And the lookout not a-looking and his pipe-bowl glowing red.

Ah! the pigtailed, quidding pirates and the pretty pranks we played,
All have since been put a stop-to by the naughty Board of Trade;
The schooners and the merry crews are laid away to rest,
A little south the sunset in the Islands of the Blest.

"The Reformed Pirate" from *The Reformed Pirate*

Frank Stockton

It was a very delightful country where little Corette lived. It seemed to be almost always summertime there, for the winters were just long enough to make people glad when they were over. When it rained, it mostly rained at night, and so the fields and gardens had all the water they wanted, while the people were generally quite sure of a fine day. And, as they lived a great deal out-of-doors, this was a great advantage to them.

The principal business of the people of this country was the raising of sweet marjoram. The soil and climate were admirably adapted to the culture of the herb, and fields and fields of it were to be seen in every direction. At that time, and this was a good while ago, very little sweet marjoram was raised in other parts of the world, so this country had the trade nearly all to itself.

The great holiday of the year was the day on which the harvest of this national herb began. It was called "Sweet Marjoram Day," and the people, both young and old, thought more of it than of any other holiday in the year.

On that happy day everybody went out into the fields. There was never a person so old, or so young, or so busy, that he or she could not go to help in the harvest. Even when there were sick people, which was seldom, they were carried out to the fields and stayed there all day. And they generally felt much better in the evening.

There were always patches of sweet marjoram planted on purpose for the very little babies to play in on the great day. They must be poor, indeed, these people said, if they could not raise sweet marjoram for their own needs and for exportation, and yet have enough left for the babies to play in.

So, all this day the little youngsters rolled and tumbled and kicked and crowed in the soft green and white beds of the fragrant herb, and pulled it up by the roots, and laughed and chuckled, and went to sleep in it, and were the happiest babies in the world.

They needed no care, except at the dinner hour, so the rest of the people gave all their time to gathering in the crop and having fun. There was always lots of fun on this great harvest day, for everybody worked so hard that the whole crop was generally in the sweet marjoram barns before breakfast, so that they had nearly the whole day for games and jollity.

In this country, where little Corette lived, there were fairies. Not very many of them, it is true, for the people had never seen but two. These were sisters, and there were never fairies more generally liked than these two little creatures, neither of them over four inches high. They were very fond of the company of human beings, and were just as full of fun as anybody. They often used to come to spend an hour or two, and sometimes a whole day, with the good folks, and they seemed always glad to see and to talk to everybody.

These sisters lived near the top of a mountain in a fairy cottage. This cottage had never been seen by any of the people, but the sisters had often told them all about it. It must have been a charming place.

The house was not much bigger than a bandbox, and it had two stories and a garret, with a little portico running all around it. Inside was the dearest little furniture of all kinds—beds, tables, chairs, and all the furniture that could possibly be needed.

Everything about the house and grounds was on the same small scale. There was a little stable and a little barn, with a little old man to work the little garden and attend to the two little cows. Around the house were garden beds ever so small, and little graveled paths; and a kitchen garden, where the peas climbed up little sticks no bigger than pins, and where the little chickens, about the size of flies, sometimes got in and scratched up the little vegetables. There was a little meadow for pasture, and a grove of little trees; and there was also a small field of sweet marjoram, where the blossoms were so tiny that you could hardly have seen them without a magnifying glass.

It was not very far from this cottage to the sweet marjoram country, and the fairy sisters had no trouble at all in running down there whenever they felt like it, but none of the people had ever seen this little home. They had looked for it, but could not find it, and the fairies would never take any of them to it. They said it was no place for human beings. Even the smallest boy, if he were to trip his toe, might fall against their house and knock it over; and as to any of them coming into the fairy grounds, that would be impossible, for there was no spot large enough for even a common-sized baby to creep about in.

On Sweet Marjoram Day the fairies never failed to come. Every year they taught the people new games, and all sorts of new ways of having fun. The good folks would never have even thought of having such fine times if it had not been for these fairies.

One delightful afternoon, about a month before Sweet Marjoram Day, Corette, who was a little girl just old enough, and not a day too old (which is exactly the age all little girls ought to be), was talking about the fairy cottage to some of her companions.

"We never can see it," said Corette, sorrowfully.

"No," said one of the other girls, "we are too big. If we were little enough, we might go."

"Are you sure the sisters would be glad to see us, then?" asked Corette.

"Yes, I heard them say so. But it doesn't matter at all, as we are not little enough."

"No," said Corette, and she went off to take a walk by herself.

She had not walked far before she reached a small house which stood by the seashore. This house belonged to a Reformed Pirate who lived there all by himself. He had entirely given up a seafaring life so as to avoid all temptation, and he employed his time in the mildest pursuits he could think of.

When Corette came to his house, she saw him sitting in an easy chair in front of his door, near the edge of a small bluff which overhung the sea, busily engaged in knitting a tidy.

When he saw Corette, he greeted her kindly, and put aside his knitting, which he was very glad to do, for he hated knitting tidies, though he thought it was his duty to make them.

"Well, my little maid," he said, in a strange, muffled voice, which sounded as if he were speaking under water, for he tried to be as gentle in every way as he could, "how do you do? You don't look quite as gay as usual. Has anything run afoul of you?"

"Oh no!" said Corette, and she came and stood by him, and taking up his tidy, she looked it over carefully and showed him where he had dropped a lot of stitches and where he had made some too tight and others a great deal too loose. He did not know how to knit very well.

When she had shown him as well as she could how he ought to do it, she sat down on the grass by his side, and after a while she began to talk to him about the fairy cottage, and what a great pity it was that it was impossible for her ever to see it.

"It *is* a pity," said the Reformed Pirate. "I've heard of that cottage, and I'd like to see it myself. In fact, I'd like to go to see almost anything that was proper and quiet, so as to get rid of the sight of this everlasting knitting."

"There are other things you might do besides knit," said Corette.

"Nothing so depressing and suitable," said he, with a sigh.

"It would be of no use for you to think of going there," said Corette. "Even I am too large, and you are ever and ever so much too big. You couldn't get one foot into any of their paths."

"I've no doubt that's true," he replied; "but the thing might be done. Almost anything can be done if you set about it in the right way. But you see, little maid, that you and I don't know enough. Now, years ago, when I was in a different line of business, I often used to get puzzled about one thing or another, and then I went to somebody who knew more than myself."

"Were there many such persons?" asked Corette.

"Well, no. I always went to one old fellow who was a Practicing Wizard. He lived, and still lives, I reckon, on an island about fifty miles from here, right off there to the sou'-sou'-west. I've no doubt that if we were to go to him, he'd tell us just how to do this thing."

"But how could we get there?" asked Corette.

"Oh! I'd manage that," said the Reformed Pirate, his eyes flashing with animation. "I've an old sailboat back there in the creek that's as good as ever she was. I could fix her up, and get everything all shipshape in a couple of days, and then you and I could scud over there in no time. What do you say? Wouldn't you like to go?"

"Oh, I'd like to go ever so much!" cried Corette, clapping her hands. "If they'd let me."

"Well, run and ask them," said he, rolling up his knitting and stuffing it under the cushion of his chair, "and I'll go and look at that boat right away."

So Corette ran home to her father and mother, and told them all about the matter. They listened with great interest, and her father said:

"Well, now, our little girl is not looking quite as well as usual. I have noticed that she is somewhat pale. A sea trip might be the very thing for her."

"I think it would do her a great deal of good," said her mother, "and as to that Reformed Pirate, she'd be just as safe with him as if she were on dry land."

So it was agreed that Corette should go. Her father and mother were always remarkably kind.

The Reformed Pirate was perfectly delighted when he heard this, and he went hard to work to get his little vessel ready. To sail again on the ocean seemed to him the greatest of earthly joys, and as he was to do it for the benefit of a good little girl, it was all perfectly right and proper.

When they started, the next day but one, all the people who lived near enough came down to see them off. Just as they were about to sail, the Reformed Pirate said:

"Hello! I wonder if I hadn't better run back to the house and get my sword! I only wear the empty scabbard now, but it might be safer, on a trip like this, to take the sword along."

So he ran back and got it, and then he pushed off amid the shouts of all the good people on the beach.

The boat was quite a good-sized one, and it had a cabin and everything neat and comfortable. The Reformed Pirate managed it beautifully, all by himself, and Corette sat and watched the waves, and the sky, and the

seabirds, and was very happy indeed.

As for her companion, he was in a state of ecstasy. As the breeze freshened, and the sails filled, and the vessel went dashing over the waves, he laughed and joked, and sang snatches of old sea songs, and was the jolliest man afloat.

After a while, as they went thus sailing merrily along, a distant ship appeared in sight. The moment his eyes fell upon it, a sudden change came over the Reformed Pirate. He sprang to his feet and, with his hand still upon the helm, he leaned forward and gazed at the ship. He gazed and he gazed, and he gazed without saying a word. Corette spoke to him several times, but he answered not. And as he gazed he moved the helm so that his little craft gradually turned from her course, and sailed to meet the distant ship.

As the two vessels approached each other, the Reformed Pirate became very much excited. He tightened his belt and loosened his sword in its sheath. Hurriedly giving the helm to Corette, he went forward and jerked a lot of ropes and hooks from a cubbyhole where they had been stowed away. Then he pulled out a small, dark flag, with bits of skeleton painted on it, and hoisted it to the topmast.

By this time he had nearly reached the ship, which was a large three-masted vessel. There seemed to be a great commotion on board; sailors were running this way and that; women were screaming; and officers could be heard shouting, "Put her about! Clap on more sail!"

But steadily on sailed the small boat, and the moment it came alongside the big ship, the Reformed Pirate threw out grapnels and made the two vessels fast together. Then he hooked a rope ladder to the side of the ship, and rushing up it, sprang with a yell on the deck of the vessel, waving his flashing sword around his head!

"Down, dastards! varlets! hounds!" he shouted. "Down upon your knees! Throw down your arms! Surrender!"

Then every man went down upon his knees, and threw down his arms and surrendered.

"Where is your Captain?" roared their conqueror.

The Captain came trembling forward.

"Bring to me your gold and silver, your jewels and your precious stones, and your rich stuffs!"

The Captain ordered these to be quickly brought and placed before the Reformed Pirate, who continued to stride to and fro across the deck waving his glittering blade, and who, when he saw the treasures placed before him, shouted again:

"Prepare for scuttling!" and then, while the women got down on their knees and begged that he would not sink the ship, and the children cried, and then men trembled so that they could hardly kneel straight, and the Captain stood pale and shaking before him, he glanced at the pile of treasure, and touched it with his sword.

"Aboard with this, my men!" he said. "But first I will divide this into— into—into *one* part. Look here!" and then he paused, glanced around, and clapped his hand to his head. He looked at the people, the treasure, and the ship. Then suddenly he sheathed his sword and, stepping up to the Captain, extended his hand.

"Good sire," said he, "you must excuse me. This is a mistake. I had no intention of taking this vessel. It was merely a temporary absence of mind. I forgot I had reformed, and seeing this ship, old scenes and my old business came into my head, and I just came and took the vessel without really thinking what I was doing. I beg you will excuse me. And these ladies—I am very sorry to have inconvenienced them. I ask them to overlook my unintentional rudeness."

"Oh, don't mention it!" cried the Captain, his face beaming with joy as he seized the hand of the Reformed Pirate. "It is of no importance, I assure

you. We are delighted, sir, delighted!"

"Oh, yes!" cried all the ladies. "Kind sir, we are charmed! We are charmed!"

"You are all very good indeed," said the Reformed Pirate, "but I really think I was not altogether excusable. And I am very sorry that I made your men bring up all these things."

"Not at all! Not at all!" cried the Captain. "No trouble whatever to show them. Very glad indeed to have the opportunity. By the by, would you like to take a few of them, as a memento of your visit?"

"Oh, no, I thank you," replied the Reformed Pirate. "I would rather not."

"Perhaps, then, some of your men might like a trinket or a bit of cloth—"

"Oh, I have no men! There is no one on board but myself—excepting a little girl, who is a passenger. But I must be going. Good-bye, Captain!"

"I am sorry you are in such a hurry," said the Captain. "Is there anything at all that I can do for you?"

"No, thank you. But stop!—there may be something. Do you sail to any port where there is a trade in tidies?"

"Oh, yes! To several such," said the Captain.

"Well, then, I would be very much obliged to you," said the Reformed Pirate, "if you would sometimes stop off that point of land that you see there, and send a boat ashore to my house for a load of tidies."

"You manufacture them by the quantity, then?" asked the Captain.

"I expect to," said the other, sadly.

The Captain promised to stop, and, after shaking hands with every person on deck, the Reformed Pirate went down the side of the ship, and taking in his ladder and his grapnels, he pushed off.

As he slowly sailed away, having lowered his flag, the Captain looked over the side of his ship, and said:

"If I had only known that there was nobody but a little girl on board! I thought, of course, he had a boatload of pirates."

"The Female Smuggler"

Collected by W. B. Whall

O come, list awhile, and you soon shall hear,
By the rolling sea lived a maiden fair.
Her father followed the smuggling trade,
Like a warlike hero.
  Like a warlike hero that never was afraid.

Now, in sailor's clothing young Jane did go,
Dressed like a sailor from top to toe;
Her aged father was the only care
O this female smuggler,
  Of this female smuggler who never did despair.

With her pistols loaded she went aboard.
And by her side hung a glittering sword,
In her belt two daggers; well armed for war
Was this female smuggler,
   Was this female smuggler, who never feared a scar.

Now they had not sail-ed far from the land,
When a strange sail brought them to a stand.
"These are sea robbers," this maid did cry,
"But the female smuggler,
   But the female smuggler will conquer or will die."

Alongside, then, this strange vessel came.
"Cheer up," cried Jane, "we will board the same;
We'll run all chances to rise or fall,"
Cried this female smuggler,
   Cried this female smuggler who never feared a ball.

Now they killed those pirates and took their store,
And soon returned to old Eng-a-land's shore.
With a keg of brandy she walked along,
Did this female smuggler,
   Did this female smuggler, and sweetly sang a song.

Now they were followed by the blockade,
Who in irons strong did put this fair maid.
But when they brought her for to be ter-ied,
This young female smuggler,
   This young female smuggler stood dress-ed like a bride.

Their commodore against her appeared,
And for her life she did greatly fear.
When he did find to his great surprise
'Twas a female smuggler,
    'Twas a female smuggler had fought him in disguise.

He to the judge and the jury said,
"I cannot prosecute this maid,
Pardon for her on my knees I crave,
For this female smuggler,
    For this female smuggler so valiant and so brave."

Then this commodore to her father went,
To gain her hand he asked his consent.
His consent he gained, so the commodore
And the female smuggler,
    And the female smuggler are one for evermore.

"Wolfert Webber, or Golden Dreams" from *Tales of a Traveller*

Washington Irving

Many months had elapsed since Wolfert Webber had frequented his old resort, the rural inn. He was taking a long lonely walk one Saturday afternoon, musing over his wants and disappointments, when his feet took instinctively their wonted direction, and on awaking out of a reverie, he found himself before the door of the inn. For some moments he hesitated whether to enter, but his heart yearned for companionship; and where can a ruined man find better companionship than at a tavern, where there is neither sober example nor sober advice to put him out of countenance?

Wolfert found several of the old frequenters of the tavern at their usual posts, and seated in their usual places; but one was missing, the great Ramm Rapelye, who for many years had filled the leather-bottomed chair of state.

His place was supplied by a stranger, who seemed, however, completely at home in the chair and the tavern. He was rather under size, but deep chested, square, and muscular. His broad shoulders, double joints, and bow knees gave tokens of prodigious strength. His face was dark and weather-beaten; a deep scar, as if from the slash of a cutlass, had almost divided his nose and made a gash in his upper lip, through which his teeth shone like a bulldog's. A mop of iron gray hair gave a grizzly finish to his hard favored visage. His dress was of an amphibious character. He wore an old hat edged with tarnished lace, and cocked in martial style, on one side of his head; a rusty blue military coat with brass buttons, and a wide pair of short petticoat trousers, or rather breeches, for they were gathered up at the knees. He ordered everybody about him with an authoritative air; talked in a brattling voice that sounded like the crackling of thorns under a pot; damned the landlord and servants with perfect impunity, and was waited upon with greater obsequiousness than had ever been shown to the mighty Ramm himself.

Wolfert's curiosity was awakened to know who and what was this stranger who had thus usurped absolute sway in this ancient domain. Peechy Prauw took him aside, into a remote corner of the hall, and there in an under voice, and with great caution, imparted to him all that he knew on the subject. The inn had been aroused several months before, on a dark stormy night, by repeated long shouts that seemed like the howlings of a wolf. They came from the water side; and at length were distinguished to be hailing the house in the seafaring manner. "House-a-hoy!" The landlord turned out with his head waiter, tapster, hostler, and errand boy—that is to say, with his old African servant Cuff. On approaching the place whence the voice proceeded, they found this amphibious-looking personage at the water's edge, quite alone, and seated on a great oaken sea chest. How he came there, whether he had been set on shore from some boat or had floated to land on his chest, nobody could tell, for he did not seem disposed to answer questions, and

there was something in his looks and manners that put a stop to all questioning. Suffice it to say, he took possession of a corner room of the inn, to which his chest was removed with great difficulty. Here he had remained ever since, keeping about the inn and its vicinity. Sometimes, it is true, he disappeared for one, two, or three days at a time, going and returning without giving any notice or account of his movement. He always appeared to have plenty of money, though often of very strange outlandish coinage; and he regularly paid his bill every evening before turning in.

He had fitted up his room to his own fancy, having slung a hammock from the ceiling instead of a bed, and decorated the walls with rusty pistols and cutlasses of foreign workmanship. A great part of his time was passed in this room, seated by the window, which commanded a wide view of the Sound, a short old fashioned pipe in his mouth, a glass of rum toddy at his elbow, and a pocket telescope in his hand, with which he reconnoitered every boat that moved upon the water. Large square-rigged vessels seemed to excite but little attention; but the moment he descried any thing with a shoulder of mutton sail, or that a barge, or yawl, or jolly boat hove in sight, up went the telescope, and he examined it with the most scrupulous attention.

All this might have passed without much notice, for in those times the province was so much the resort of adventurers of all characters and climes that any oddity in dress or behavior attracted but small attention. In a little while, however, this strange sea monster, thus strangely cast up on dry land, began to encroach upon the long-established customs and customers of the place, and to interfere in a dictatorial manner in the affairs of the ninepin alley and the barroom, until in the end he usurped an absolute command over the whole inn. It was all in vain to attempt to withstand his authority. He was not exactly quarrelsome, but boisterous and peremptory, like one accustomed to tyrannize on a quarterdeck; and there was a daredevil air about everything he said and did, that inspired a wariness in all bystanders.

Even the half-pay officer, so long the hero of the club, was soon silenced by him; and the quiet burghers stared with wonder at seeing their inflammable man of war so readily and quietly extinguished.

And then the tales that he would tell were enough to make a peaceable man's hair stand on end. There was not a sea fight, or marauding, or freebooting adventure that had happened within the last twenty years but he seemed perfectly versed in it. He delighted to talk of the exploits of the buccaneers in the West Indies and on the Spanish Main. How his eyes would glisten as he described the waylaying of treasure ships, the desperate fights, yardarm and yardarm—broadside and broadside—the boarding and capturing of huge Spanish galleons! With what chuckling relish would he describe the descent upon some rich Spanish colony; the rifling of a church; the sacking of a convent! You would have thought you heard some gormandizer dilating upon the roasting of a savory goose at Michaelmas as he described the roasting of some Spanish Don to make him discover his treasure—a detail given with a minuteness that made every rich old burgher present turn uncomfortably in his chair. All this would be told with infinite glee, as if he considered it an excellent joke; and then he would give such a tyrannical leer in the face of his next neighbor, that the poor man would be fain to laugh out of sheer faintheartedness. If any one, however, pretended to contradict him in any of his stories, he was on fire in an instant. His very cocked hat assumed a momentary fierceness, and seemed to resent the contradiction. "How the devil should you know as well as I! I tell you it was as I say!" And he would at the same time let slip a broadside of thundering oaths and tremendous sea phrases, such as had never been heard before within those peaceful walls.

Indeed, the worthy burghers began to surmise that he knew more of these stories than mere hearsay. Day after day their conjectures concerning him grew more and more wild and fearful. The strangeness of his arrival, the strangeness of his manners, the mystery that surrounded him, all made him something incomprehensible in their eyes. He was a kind of monster of the deep to them—he was a merman—he was behemoth—he was leviathan—in short they knew not what he was.

The domineering spirit of this boisterous sea urchin at length grew quite intolerable. He was no respecter of persons; he contradicted the richest burghers without hesitation; he took possession of the sacred elbow chair, which time out of mind had been the seat of sovereignty of the illustrious Ramm Rapelye. Nay, he even went so far, in one of his rough jocular moods, as to slap that mighty burgher on the back, drink his toddy, and wink in his face, a thing scarcely to be believed. From this time Ramm Rapelye appeared no more at the inn; his example was followed by several of the most eminent customers, who were too rich to tolerate being bullied out of their opinions or being obliged to laugh at another man's jokes. The landlord was almost in despair, but he knew not how to get rid of this sea monster and his sea chest, which seemed both to have grown like fixtures, or excrescences on his establishment.

Such was the account whispered cautiously in Wolfert's ear, by the narrator, Peechy Prauw, as he held him by the button in the corner of the hall, casting a wary glance now and then toward the door of the barroom, lest he should be overheard by the terrible hero of his tale.

Wolfert took his seat in a remote part of the room in silence; impressed with profound awe of this unknown, so versed in freebooting history. It was to him a wonderful instance of the revolutions of mighty empires, to find the venerable Ramm Rapelye thus ousted from the throne, and a rugged tarpaulin dictating from his elbow chair, hectoring the patriarchs, and filling this tranquil little realm with brawl and bravado.

The stranger was on this evening in a more than usually communicative mood, and was narrating a number of astounding stories of plunderings and burnings upon the high seas. He dwelt upon them with peculiar relish, heightening the frightful particulars in proportion to their effect on his peaceful auditors. He gave a swaggering detail of the capture of a Spanish merchantman. She was lying becalmed during a long summer's day, just off from an island which was one of the lurking places of the pirates. They had reconnoitered her with their spyglasses from the shore, and ascertained her character and force. At night a picked crew of daring fellows set off for her in a whaleboat. They approached with muffled oars, as she lay rocking idly with the undulations of the sea and her sails flapping against the masts. They were close under her stern before the guard on deck was aware of their approach. The alarm was given; the pirates threw hand grenades on deck and sprang up the main chains sword in hand.

The crew flew to arms, but in great confusion; some were shot down, others took refuge in the tops; others were driven overboard and drowned, while others fought hand to hand from the main deck to the quarterdeck, disputing gallantly every inch of ground. There were three Spanish gentlemen on board with their ladies, who made the most desperate resistance. They defended the companionway, cut down several of their assailants, and fought like very devils, for they were maddened by the shrieks of the ladies from the cabin. One of the Dons was old and soon dispatched. The other two kept their ground vigorously, even though the captain of the pirates was among their assailants. Just then there was a shout of victory from the main deck. "The ship is ours!" cried the pirates.

One of the Dons immediately dropped his sword and surrendered; the other, who was a hotheaded youngster, and just married, gave the captain a slash in the face that laid all open. The captain just made out to articulate the words "no quarter."

"And what did they do with their prisoners?" said Peechy Prauw, eagerly.

"Threw them all overboard!" was the answer.

A dead pause followed this reply. Peechy Prauw shrunk quietly back like a man who had unwarily stolen upon the lair of a sleeping lion. The honest burghers cast fearful glances at the deep scar slashed across the visage of the stranger and moved their chairs a little farther off. The seaman, however, smoked on without moving a muscle, as though he either did not perceive or did not regard the unfavorable effect he had produced upon his hearers.

The half-pay officer was the first to break the silence; for he was continually tempted to make ineffectual head against this tyrant of the seas, and to regain his lost consequence in the eyes of his ancient companions. He now tried to match the gunpowder tales of the stranger by others equally tremendous. Kidd, as usual, was his hero, concerning whom he seemed to have picked up many of the floating traditions of the province. The seaman had always evinced a settled pique against the one-eyed warrior. On this occasion he listened with peculiar impatience. He sat with one arm akimbo, the other elbow on a table, the hand holding on to the small pipe he was pettishly puffing; his legs crossed, drumming with one foot on the ground and casting every now and then the side glance of a basilisk at the prosing captain. At length the latter spoke of Kidd's having ascended the Hudson with some of his crew, to land his plunder in secrecy.

"Kidd up the Hudson!" burst forth the seaman, with a tremendous oath; "Kidd never was up the Hudson!"

"I tell you he was," said the other. "Aye, and they say he buried a quantity of treasure on the little flat that runs out into the river, called the Devil's Dans Kammer."

"The Devil's Dans Kammer in your teeth!" cried the seaman. "I tell you, Kidd never was up the Hudson—what a plague do you know of Kidd and his haunts?"

"What do I know?" echoed the half-pay officer. "Why, I was in London

at the time of his trial, aye, and I had the pleasure of seeing him hanged at Execution Dock."

"Then, sir, let me tell you that you saw as pretty a fellow hanged as ever trod shoe leather. Aye!" putting his face nearer to that of the officer, "and there was many a landlubber looked on, that might much better have swung in his stead."

The half-pay officer was silenced; but the indignation thus pent up in his bosom glowed with intense vehemence in his single eye, which kindled like a coal.

Peechy Prauw, who never could remain silent, observed that the gentleman certainly was in the right. Kidd never did bury money up the Hudson, nor indeed in any of those parts, though many affirmed such to be the fact. It was Bradish and others of the buccaneers who had buried money, some said in Turtle Bay, others on Long Island, others in the neighborhood of Hell Gate. Indeed, added he, I recollect an adventure of Sam, the African fisherman, many years ago, which some think had something to do with the buccaneers. As we are all friends here, and as it will go no farther, I'll tell it to you.

"Upon a dark night many years ago, as Black Sam was returning from fishing in Hell Gate—"

Here the story was nipped in the bud by a sudden movement from the unknown, who laying his iron fist on the table, knuckles downward, with a quiet force that indented the very boards, and looking grimly over his shoulder, with the grin of an angry bear. "Heark'ee, neighbor," said he, with significant nodding of the head, "you'd better let the buccaneers and their money alone—they're not for old men and old women to meddle with. They fought hard for their money, they gave body and soul for it, and wherever it lies buried, depend upon it he must have a tug with the devil who gets it."

This sudden explosion was succeeded by a blank silence throughout the room. Peechy Prauw shrunk within himself, and even the one-eyed officer turned pale. Wolfert, who from a dark corner of the room, had listened with intense eagerness to all this talk about buried treasure, looked with mingled awe and reverence on this bold buccaneer, for such he really suspected him to be. There was a chinking of gold and sparkling of jewels in all his stories about the Spanish Main that gave a value to every period, and Wolfert would have given anything for the rummaging of the ponderous sea chest, which his imagination crammed full of golden chalices and crucifixes and jolly round bags of doubloons.

The dead stillness that had fallen upon the company was at length interrupted by the stranger, who pulled out a prodigious watch of curious and ancient workmanship, and which in Wolfert's eyes had a decidedly Spanish look. On touching a spring it struck ten o'clock; upon which the sailor called for his reckoning, and having paid it out of a handful of outlandish coin, he drank off the remainder of his beverage, and without taking leave of anyone, rolled out of the room, muttering to himself, as he stumped upstairs to his chamber.

It was some time before the company could recover from the silence into which they had been thrown. The very footsteps of the stranger, which were heard now and then as he traversed his chamber, inspired awe.

Still the conversation in which they had been engaged was too interesting not to be resumed. A heavy thunder gust had gathered up unnoticed while they were lost in talk, and the torrents of rain that fell forbade all thoughts of setting off for home until the storm should subside. They drew nearer together, therefore, and entreated the worthy Peechy Prauw to continue the tale which had been so discourteously interrupted. He readily complied, whispering, however, in a tone scarcely above his breath, and drowned occasionally by the rolling of the thunder; and he would pause every now and then, and listen with evident awe, as he heard the heavy footsteps of the stranger pacing overhead.

Lyrics from "The Buccaneer"

John Masefield

I

We are far from sight of the harbor lights,
   Of the seaports whence we came,
But the old sea calls and the cold wind bites,
   And our hearts are turned to flame.

And merry and rich is the goodly gear
   We'll win upon the tossing sea,
A silken gown for my dainty dear,
   And a gold doubloon for me.

It's the old old road and the old old quest
   Of the cutthroat sons of Cain,

South by west and a quarter west,
    And hey for the Spanish Main.

II

There's a sea-way somewhere where all day long
    Is the hushed susurrus of the sea,
The mewing of the skuas, and the sailor's song,
    And the wind's cry calling me.

There's a haven somewhere where the quiet of the bay
    Is troubled with the shifting tide,
Where the gulls are flying, crying in the bright white spray,
    And the tan-sailed schooners ride.

III

The toppling rollers at the harbor mouth
    Are spattering the bows with foam,
And the anchor's catted, and she's heading for the south
    With her topsails sheeted home.

And a merry measure is the dance she'll tread
    (To the clanking of the staysail's hanks)
When the guns are growling and the blood runs red,
    And the prisoners are walking of the planks.

"Tom Chist and the Treasure Box" from *Tales of Pirates and Buccaneers*

Howard Pyle

To tell about Tom Chist, and how he got his name, and how he came to be living at the little settlement of Henlopen just inside the mouth of Delaware Bay, the story must begin as far back as 1686, when a great storm swept the Atlantic coast from end to end. During the heaviest part of the hurricane a boat went ashore on the Hen-and-Chicken Shoals, just below Cape Henlopen and at the mouth of Delaware Bay, and Tom Chist was the only soul of all those on board the ill-fated vessel who escaped alive.

This story must first be told, since it was because of his strange and miraculous escape at that time that he gained the name given to him.

This wreck was a godsend to the poor and needy settlers in the wilderness where so few good things ever came. For the vessel went to pieces during the night, and the next morning the beach was strewn with wreckage—boxes and barrels, chests and poles, timbers and planks, a plentiful and bountiful harvest to be gathered up by the settlers as they chose, with no one to forbid or prevent them.

The name of the boat, as found painted on some of the water barrels and sea chests, was the *Bristol Merchant*, and she presumedly hailed from England.

And the only soul who escaped alive from the wreck was Tom Chist.

A settler, a fisherman named Matt Abrahamson, and his daughter Molly found Tom. He was washed up on the beach among the wreckage, in a great wooden box which had been securely tied around with a rope and lashed between two poles—apparently for better protection in beating through the surf. Matt Abrahamson thought he had found something of more than usual value when he came upon this chest. But when he cut the cords and broke open the box with his ax, he could not have been more astonished: he beheld a baby, nine or ten months old, lying half smothered in the blankets that covered the bottom of the box.

Matt Abrahamson's daughter Molly's own baby had died a month or so before. So when she saw the little one lying there in the bottom of the chest, she cried out in a loud voice that the Good Man had sent her another baby in place of her own.

The rain was driving before the hurricane storm in dim, slanting sheets, and so she wrapped up the baby in the man's coat she wore, and ran off home without waiting to gather up any more of the wreckage.

It was Parson Hillary Jones who gave the foundling his name. When the news came to his ears of what Matt Abrahamson had found, he went over to the fisherman's cabin to see the child. He examined the clothes in which the baby was dressed. They were of fine linen and handsomely stitched, and the reverend gentleman's opinion was that the foundling's parents must have

been well off. A kerchief had been wrapped around the baby's neck and under its arms and tied behind, and in the corner, marked with very fine needlework, were the initials "T.C."

"What d'ye call him, Molly?" said Parson Jones. He was standing, as he spoke, with his back to the fire, warming his palms before the blaze. The pocket of the greatcoat he wore bulged out with a big bottle of spirits which he had taken from the wreck that afternoon. "What d'ye call him, Molly?"

"I'll call him Tom, after my own baby."

"That goes very well with the initial on the kerchief," said Parson Jones. "But what other name d'ye give him? Let it be something to go with the C."

"I don't know," said Molly.

"Why not call him Chist, since he was born in a chist out of the sea? 'Tom Chist'—the name goes off like a flash in the pan." And so Tom Chist he was called, and Tom Chist he was christened.

So much for the beginning of the history of Tom Chist. The story of Captain Kidd's treasure box does not begin until the late spring of 1699.

That was the year that the famous pirate captain, coming up from the West Indies, sailed his sloop into Delaware Bay, where he lay for over a month waiting for news from his friends in New York.

For he had sent word to that town asking if the coast was clear for him to return home with the rich prize he had brought from the Indian seas and the coast of Africa, and meantime he lay there in Delaware Bay waiting for his reply. Before he left, he turned the whole of Tom Chist's life topsy-turvy with something that he brought ashore.

Besides his foster mother, Tom Chist had a very good friend in Parson Jones, who used to come over every now and then to Abrahamson's hut hoping to get a half-dozen fish for breakfast. He always had a kind word or two for Tom, who during the winter evenings would go over to the good man's house to learn his letters, and to read and write and cipher a little, so that by now he was able to spell the words out of the Bible and the almanac and even knew some arithmetic.

This is the sort of boy Tom Chist was, and this is the sort of life he led. In the late spring or early summer of 1699, Captain Kidd's sloop sailed into the mouth of Delaware Bay and changed the whole fortune of his life.

And this is the story of Captain Kidd's treasure box:

Old Matt Abrahamson kept the flat-bottomed boat in which he went out fishing some distance down the shore, and in the neighborhood of the old wreck that had been sunk on the shoals. This was the usual fishing ground of the settlers, and here old Matt's boat generally lay drawn up on the sand.

There had been a thunderstorm that afternoon, and Tom had gone down the beach to bail out the boat against the morning's fishing. It was an evening full of moonlight now, as he was returning, and the night sky was filled with floating clouds. Now and then there was a dull flash to the west, and once a muttering growl of thunder, promising another storm to come.

All that day the pirate sloop had been lying just off the shore at the back of the capes, and now Tom Chist could see the sails glimmering in the moonlight, spread for drying after the storm. He was walking up the shore homeward when he became aware that at some distance ahead of him there was a boat drawn up on the little narrow beach; a group of men were clustered around it. He hurried forward with a good deal of curiosity to see who had landed, but it was not until he had come close to them that he could distinguish who and what they were. Then he knew that it must be a party that had come from the pirate sloop. They had evidently just landed, and two men were lifting out a chest from the boat. One of them was a black man, naked to the waist, and the other was a white man in his shirtsleeves, wearing petticoat breeches, a Monteray cap on his head, a red bandanna kerchief around his neck, and gold earrings in his ears. He had a long braid of

hair hanging down his back and a great sheath-knife dangling from his side. Another man, evidently the captain of the party, stood a little distance away as they lifted the chest out of the boat. He had a cane in one hand and a lit lantern in the other, although the moon was shining as bright as day. He wore jackboots and a handsome laced coat, and he had a long drooping mustache that curled down below his chin. He wore a fine feathered hat, and his long black hair hung down upon his shoulders.

They were so busy lifting the chest from the boat that at first they did not observe that Tom Chist had come up and was standing there. It was the man with the long braid and the gold earrings that spoke to him. "Boy, what do you want here, boy?" he said, in a rough, hoarse voice. "Where d'ye come from?" And then dropping his end of the chest, and without giving Tom time to answer, he pointed off down the beach, and said, "You'd better be going about your own business, if you know what's good for you. And don't you come back, or you'll find what you don't want waiting for you."

Tom saw in a glance that the pirates were all looking at him, and then, without saying a word, he turned and walked away. The man who had spoken to him followed him threateningly for a short distance, as though to see that he had gone away as he was told to do. But soon he stopped, and Tom hurried on alone, until the boat and the crew and all were lost in the moonlit night. Then he himself stopped also, turned, and looked back toward where he had left.

There had been something very strange in the appearance of the men he had just seen, something very mysterious in their actions, and he wondered what it all meant, and what they were going to do. He stood for a little while looking and listening. He could see nothing, and could hear only the sound of distant talking. What were they doing on the lonely shore at night? Then, following a sudden impulse, he turned and cut off across the sand humps, skirting around inland, but keeping pretty close to the shore; his object was to spy upon them and to watch what they were doing from the back of the sand hills that fronted the beach.

He had gone along some distance when he became aware of the sound of voices that seemed to be drawing closer to him as he came toward the speakers. He stopped and stood listening, and instantly as he stopped, the voices stopped also. He crouched there silently in the bright, glimmering moonlight, surrounded by the silent stretches of sand, and the stillness seemed to press upon him like a heavy hand. Then suddenly the sound of a man's voice began again, and as Tom listened he could hear someone slowly counting. "Ninety-one," the voice began, "ninety-two, ninety-three, ninety-four," and so on with the slow, monotonous count coming nearer and nearer to him.

Suddenly he saw three heads appear above the sand hill, so close to him that he crouched down quickly with a keen thrill, beside the mound near which he stood. His first fear was that they might have seen him in the moonlight; but they had not, and his heart rose again as the counting voice went steadily on. "One hundred and twenty," it was saying, "and twenty-one, and twenty-two, and twenty-three, and twenty-four," and then he who was counting came out from behind the little sandy rise into the white and open level of shimmering brightness.

It was the man with the cane whom Tom had seen some time before—the captain of the party that had landed. He carried his cane under his arm now, and was holding his lantern close to something that he held in his hand, and upon which he looked narrowly as he walked with a slow and measured tread in a perfectly straight line across the sand, counting each step as he took it.

Behind him walked two other figures, the ones whom Tom had seen lifting the chest out of the boat. Now they were carrying the heavy box between them, laboring through the sand with shuffling steps as they bore it onward.

As he who was counting pronounced the word "thirty," the two men set the chest down on the sand with a grunt, the man with the earrings panting and blowing and wiping his sleeve across his forehead. And immediately he who counted took out a slip of paper and marked something down upon it. They stood there for a long time, during which Tom lay behind the sand hill watching them, and for a while the silence was uninterrupted. In the perfect stillness Tom could hear the washing of the little waves beating upon the distant beach, and once the faraway sound of a laugh from one of those who stood by the boat.

One, two, three minutes passed, and then the men picked up the chest and started on again; and then again the other man began his counting, still looking intently at that which he held in his hand—until the three figures disappeared in the little hollow between the two sand hills on the opposite side of the open, and still Tom could hear the sound of the counting voice in the distance.

Just as they disappeared behind the hill, there was a sudden faint flash of light; and as Tom lay still listening to the counting, he heard, after a long interval, a faraway muffled rumble of distant thunder. He waited for a while, and then arose and stepped to the top of the sand hill behind which he had been lying. He looked all about him, but there was no one else to be seen. Then he stepped down from the mound and followed in the direction in which the pirate captain and the two men carrying the chest had gone. He crept along cautiously, stopping now and then to make sure that he still heard the counting voice, and when it ceased he laid down upon the sand and waited until it began again.

So following the pirates, he saw the three figures again in the distance, and, skirting around the back of a hill of sand covered with coarse grass, he came to where he overlooked a little open, level space gleaming white in the moonlight.

The three had been crossing the level of sand and were now not more than twenty-five paces from him. They had again set down the chest, upon which the white man with the long braid and the gold earrings had seated to rest himself, the black man standing close beside him. The moon shone as bright as day and fully upon his face. It was looking directly at Tom Chist, every line as keenly cut with white lights and black shadows as though it had been carved in ivory and ebony. He sat perfectly motionless, and Tom drew back, startled, almost thinking he had been discovered. He lay silent, his heart beating heavily in his throat; but there was no alarm, and soon he heard the counting begin again, and when he looked once more, he saw they were going away, straight across the little open. A soft, sliding hill of sand lay directly in front of them. They did not turn aside but went straight over it, the leader helping himself up the sandy slope with his cane, still counting, and still keeping his eyes fixed upon that which he held in his hand. Then they disappeared again behind the white crest on the other side.

So Tom followed them cautiously until they had gone almost half a mile inland. When he saw them clearly again, it was from a little grassy rise which looked down like the crest of a bowl upon the floor of sand below. Upon this smooth white floor the moon beat with almost dazzling brightness.

The white man who had helped to carry the chest was now kneeling, busy at some work, though what it was Tom at first could not see. He was whittling the point of a stick into a long wooden peg, and when he had finished what he was doing, he arose and stepped to where he who seemed to be the captain had stuck his cane upright into the ground, as though to mark some particular spot. He drew the cane out of the sand, thrusting the stick down in its stead. Then he drove the long peg down with a wooden mallet which the black man handed to him. The sharp rapping of the mallet upon the top of the peg sounded loud in the perfect stillness, and Tom lay watching and wondering what it all meant. The man, with quick repeated blows,

drove the peg further and further down into the sand until it showed only two or three inches above the surface. As he finished his work, there was another faint flash of light, and then another smothered rumble of thunder; Tom, as he looked out toward the west, saw the silver rim of the round and sharply outlined thundercloud rising slowly up into the sky and pushing the other broken, drifting clouds before it.

The two white men were now stooping over the peg, the black man watching them. Then the man with the cane began walking straight away from the peg, carrying the end of the measuring line with him, the other end of which the man with the earrings held against the top of the peg. When the pirate captain had reached the end of the measuring line, he marked a cross upon the sand, and then again they measured out another stretch of space.

So they measured a distance five times over, and then, from where Tom lay, he could see the man with the braid drive another peg just at the foot of a sloping rise of sand that beyond swept up into a tall white dune that appeared sharp and clear against the night sky. As soon as the man with the braid had driven the second peg into the ground, they began measuring again. And so, still measuring, they disappeared in another direction which took them in behind the sand dune, where Tom no longer could see what they were doing.

The black man still sat by the chest where the two had left him, only now he was looking all around him, and so bright and strong was the moonlight that from where he lay Tom could see the glint of it twinkling in his eyes.

Then from behind the hill there came, for the third time, the sharp rapping sound of the mallet driving still another peg, and after a while the two pirates emerged from behind the sloping whiteness into the space of moonlight again.

They came directly to where the chest lay. The white man and the black man lifting it once more, they walked across the level of open sand, and then on behind the edge of the hill and out of Tom's sight.

Tom Chist could no longer see what the pirates were doing; neither did he dare to cross over the open space of sand that now lay between them and him. He lay there speculating as to what was going on, and meantime the storm cloud was rising higher and higher above the horizon, with louder and louder mutterings of thunder following each dull flash from out of the cavernous cloudy depths. In the silence he could hear an occasional click, as of some iron implement, and he thought that the pirates were burying the chest, though just where they were at work he could neither see nor tell.

Still he lay there watching and listening, and soon a puff of warm air blew across the sand, and a thumping tumble of louder thunder leaped from out the belly of the storm cloud, which every minute was coming nearer and nearer. Still Tom Chist lay watching.

Suddenly, almost unexpectedly to him, the three figures reappeared from behind the sand hill, the pirate captain leading the way, his two associates following closely behind him. They had gone just about halfway across the sandy level between the hill and the mound behind which Tom Chist lay, when the pirate with the earrings stopped and bent over as though to tie his shoe. This brought the black man a few steps in front of his companion.

That which then followed happened so suddenly, so unexpectedly, so swiftly, that Tom Chist had hardly time to realize what it all meant before it was over. As the black pirate passed him, the other man arose suddenly and silently erect, and Tom Chist saw the white moonlight glint upon the blade of a long knife which he now held in his hand. He took one, two silent, cat-like steps, and then there was a sweeping flash of the blade in the moonlight, and a blow, the thump of which Tom could distinctly hear even from where he lay stretched out upon the sand. There was an instant echoing yell from the stricken man, who ran stumbling forward, stopped, regained his footing, and then stood for an instant as though rooted to the spot.

Tom had distinctly seen the knife enter his back, and even thought that he had seen the glint of the point as it came out from the chest. Meantime the pirate captain had stopped, and now stood with his hand resting upon his cane looking calmly on.

The pirate with the braid stood for a while staring at the wounded man, who was now some distance away, and who was not very far from Tom when he staggered and fell. He tried to rise, then fell forward again, and then lay still. At that instant the first edge of the cloud cut across the moon, and there was a sudden darkness; but in the silence Tom heard the sound of another blow and a groan, and then a voice calling to the pirate captain that it was all over.

He saw the dim form of the captain crossing the level sand, and then, as the moon sailed out from behind the cloud, he saw one man standing over a figure that lay motionless upon the sand.

Then Tom Chist scrambled up and ran away, plunging down into the hollow of sand that lay in the shadows below. Over the next rise he ran, and down again into the next black hollow, and so on over the sliding, shifting ground, panting and gasping. It seemed to him that he could hear footsteps following, and in the dreadful terror that possessed him he almost expected at any moment to feel the cold knife-blade slide between his own ribs in such a thrust from behind as he had seen given to the poor victim.

He ran on, all the way to the parson's house, hardly stopping once in all the way, and when he knocked at the door he was panting and sobbing for breath.

The good man was sitting on the back-kitchen doorstep smoking his long pipe.

Tom Chist never could tell how he got his story told, but somehow, in convulsive fits and starts, panting and gasping for breath, he did manage to tell it all.

Parson Jones listened with breathless and perfect silence, broken only now and then by inarticulate sounds.

"And I don't know why they should have killed the poor black man," said Tom, as he finished his narrative.

"Why, that is very easy enough to understand," said the good reverend. "'Twas a treasure box they buried, Tom. A treasure box! A treasure box!"

In his excitement Mr. Jones had got up from his seat and was stamping up and down, puffing out great clouds of tobacco smoke into the hot air.

"A treasure box?" cried out Tom.

"Ay, a treasure box! And that was why they killed the poor black man. He was the only one, d'ye see, besides they two who knew the place where 'twas hid, and now that they've killed him out of the way, there's nobody but themselves knows. The villains— Tut, tut, look at that, now!" In his excitement the parson had snapped the stem of his pipe in two.

"Why, then," said Tom, "if that is so, 'tis indeed a wicked, bloody treasure, and fit to bring a curse upon anybody who finds it!"

"'Tis more likely to bring a curse upon the soul who buried it," said Parson Jones. "And it may be a blessing to him who finds it. But tell me, Tom, do you think you could find the place again where 'twas hid?"

"I can't tell that," said Tom. "'Twas all among the sand hills, d'ye see, and it was night as well. But I could find the place where the boat was drawn up on the beach."

"Why, then, that's something to start from, Tom," said his friend, "If we can find that, then maybe we can find where they went from there."

"If I was certain it was a treasure box," cried out Tom Chist, "I would rake over every foot of sand between here and Henlopen to find it."

"'Twould be like hunting for a needle in a haystack," said the Reverend Hillary Jones.

As Tom walked home, it seemed not only as though a ton's weight of gloom had been rolled away from his soul, but as though he could hardly contain himself with the prospect of treasure-hunting to look forward to.

The next day, early in the afternoon, Parson Jones and Tom Chist started off together, Tom carrying a spade over his shoulder, and the reverend gentleman walking along with his cane. As they jogged up the beach, they talked together about the only thing they could talk about—the treasure box. "And how big did you say 'twas?" asked the good gentleman.

"About so long," said Tom Chist, measuring off upon the spade, "and about so wide and this deep."

"And what if it should be full of money, Tom?" said the reverend gentleman, swinging his cane around and around in wide circles in the excitement of the thought, as he strode along briskly. "Suppose it should be full of money, what then?"

"By Moses!" said Tom Chist, hurrying to keep up with his friend. "I'd buy a ship for myself, I would, and I'd trade with India and with China, I would. Suppose the chist was all full of money, sir, and suppose we should find it—would there be enough in it, d'ye suppose to buy a ship?"

"To be sure there would be enough, Tom; enough and to spare, and a good big lump over."

"And if I find it, 'tis mine to keep, is it, and no mistake?"

"Why, to be sure it would be yours!" cried out the parson, in a loud voice. "To be sure it would be yours!" He knew nothing of the laws, but the doubt of the question began at once to ferment in his brain, and he strode along in silence for a while. "Whose else would it be but yours if you find it?" he burst out. "Can you tell me that?"

"If ever I have a ship of my own," said Tom Chist, "and if ever I sail to India in her, I'll fetch ye back the best chist of tea, sir, that ever was fetched from China."

Parson Jones burst out laughing. "Thankee, Tom," he said, "and I'll thankee again when I get my chist of tea. But tell me, Tom, didst thou ever hear of the farmer girl who counted her chickens before they were hatched?"

It was thus they talked as they hurried along up the beach together, and so came to a place at last where Tom stopped short and stood looking about him. "'Twas just here," he said, "I saw the boat last night. Ay, I know 'twas here, for I remember that bit of wreck yonder, and that there was a tall stake drove in the sand just where that stake stands."

Parson Jones put on his spectacles and went over to the stake toward which Tom pointed. As soon as he had looked at it carefully, he called out: "Why, Tom, this hath just been driven down into the sand. 'Tis a brand-new stake of wood, and the pirates must have set it here themselves as a mark, just as they drove the pegs you spoke about down into the sand."

Tom came over and looked at the stake. It was a stout piece of oak nearly two inches thick; it had been shaped with some care, and the top of it had been painted red. He shook the stake and tried to move it, but it had been driven or planted so deeply into the sand that he could not stir it.

"Ay, sir," he said, "it must have been set here for a mark, for I'm sure 'twas not here yesterday or the day before." He stood looking all around him to see if there were other signs of the pirates' presence. At some distance away there was the corner of something white sticking up out of the sand. He could see that it was a scrap of paper, and he pointed to it, calling out, "There's a piece of paper over there, sir. I wonder if they left that behind?"

If he had only known the miraculous chance that placed that paper there, he would not have walked over to it as carelessly as he did to pluck it up out of the sand. There was only an inch of it showing, and if it had not been for his sharp eyes, it would certainly have been overlooked and passed by. The next windstorm would have covered it up, and all that afterward happened never would have happened. "Look, sir," he said, as he struck the sand from it, "it has writing on it."

"Let me see it," said Parson Jones. He adjusted the spectacles a little more firmly on his nose as he took the paper in his hand and began reading it. "What's all this?" he said. "A whole lot of figures and nothing else." And then he read aloud. "'Mark—S–SW by S'. What d'ye suppose that means, Tom?"

"I don't know, sir," said Tom. "But maybe we can understand it better if we read on."

"'Tis all a great lot of figures," said Parson Jones, "without a grain of meaning in them so far as I can see, unless they be sailing directions." And then he began reading again until he came to "Peg. S–SW by S 427 foot. Peg. Dig to the west of this six foot."

"What's that about a peg?" exclaimed Tom. "What's that about a peg? And then there's something about digging too!" It was as though a sudden light began shining into his brain. He felt himself growing quickly very excited. "Read that over again, sir," he cried. "Why, sir, you remember I told you they drove a peg into the sand. And don't they say to dig close to it? Read it over again, sir—read it over again!"

"Peg?" said the good gentleman. "To be sure it was about a peg. Let's look again. Yes, here it is. 'Peg. SE by E 269 foot.'"

"Ay!" cried out Tom Chist again, in great excitement. "Don't you remember what I told you, sir, 269 foot? Surely that must be what I saw 'em measuring with the line."

Parson Jones had now caught the flame of excitement that began to blaze up so strongly in Tom's breast. He felt as though some wonderful thing was about to happen to them. "To be sure, to be sure!" he called out in a great

big voice. "And then they measured out 427 foot west by south, and then they drove another peg, and then they buried the box six foot to the west of it. Why, Tom—why, Tom Chist! If we've read this right, thy fortune is made."

Tom Chist stood staring straight at the old gentleman's excited face, seeing nothing but it in all the bright infinity of sunshine. Were they indeed about to find the treasure chest? He felt the sun very hot upon his shoulders, and he heard the harsh, insistent jarring of a tern that hovered and circled with forked tail and sharp white wings in the sunlight just above their heads. But all the time he stood staring into the good old gentleman's face.

It was Parson Jones who first spoke. "But what do all these figures mean?" And Tom observed how the paper shook and rustled in the tremor of excitement that shook his hand. He raised the paper to the focus of his spectacles and began to read again. "'Mark. 40, 72, 91—'"

"Mark?" cried out Tom, almost screaming. "Why, that must mean the stake yonder; that must be the mark." And he pointed to the oak stick with its red tip blazing against the white shimmer of sand behind it.

"And the 40 and 72 and 91," cried the old gentleman, in a voice equally shrill, "why, that must mean the number of steps the pirate was counting when you heard him."

"To be sure, that's what they mean!" cried Tom Chist. "That is it, and it can be nothing else. Oh, come, sir—come, sir; let us make haste and find it!"

"Wait, wait!" said the good gentleman, holding up his hand; and again Tom Chist noticed how it trembled and shook. His voice was steady enough, though very hoarse, but his hand shook and trembled. "Wait! First of all, we must follow these measurements. And 'tis a marvelous thing," he croaked, after a little pause, "how this paper ever came to be here."

"Maybe it was blown here by the wind," suggested Tom Chist.

"Likely enough, likely enough," said Parson Jones. "Likely enough, after the wretches had buried the chest and killed that poor man, they were so elated by their wicked deeds that, when it dropped out of the man's pocket, it blew away from him without his knowing it."

"But let us find the box!" cried out Tom Chist, squirming in his excitement.

"Ay, ay," said the good man, "only wait a moment, my boy, until we make sure what we're doing. I've got my pocket-compass here, but we must have something to measure off the feet when we have found the peg. You run across to Tom Brooke's house and fetch that measuring rod he used to lay out his new barn. While you're gone, I'll pace off the distance marked on the paper with my pocket-compass."

Tom Chist was gone for almost an hour, though he ran nearly all the way there and back, borne on the wings of his excitement. When he returned, panting, Parson Jones was nowhere to be seen, but Tom saw his footsteps leading away inland, and he followed the scuffling marks in the smooth surface across the sand humps and down into the hollows, and soon he found the good gentleman in a spot he at once knew as soon as he laid his eyes upon it.

It was the open space where the pirates had driven their first peg, and where Tom Chist had afterward seen them kill the poor black man. Tom Chist gazed around as though expecting to see some sign of the tragedy, but the space was as smooth and as undisturbed as a floor, except where, midway across it, Parson Jones, who was now stooping over something on the ground, had trampled on it.

When Tom Chist saw him, he was still bending over, scraping the sand away from something he had found.

It was the first peg!

Within half an hour they had found the second and third pegs, and Tom Chist stripped off his coat and began digging like mad down into the sand, Parson Jones standing over him and watching. The sun was sloping more than halfway toward the west when the blade of Tom Chist's spade struck something hard.

If it had been his own heart that he had hit in the sand, his breast could hardly have been more thrilled.

It was the treasure box!

Parson Jones himself leaped down into the hole and began scraping away the sand with his hands as though he had gone crazy. At last, with some difficulty, they tugged and hauled the chest up out of the sand to the surface, where it lay covered all over with the grit that clung to it.

It was securely locked and fastened with a padlock, and it took a good many blows with the blade of the spade to burst the bolt. Parson Jones himself lifted the lid.

Tom Chist leaned forward and gazed down into the open box. He would not have been surprised to have seen it filled full of yellow gold and bright jewels. It was half full of books and papers, and half full of canvas bags tied safely and securely with cords of string.

Parson Jones lifted out one of the bags, and it jingled as he did so. It was full of money.

He cut the string, and with trembling, shaking hands, handed the bag to Tom, who, in an ecstasy of wonder and dizzy delight, poured out with swimming sight upon the coat spread on the ground a mass of shining silver money that rang and twinkled and jingled as it fell in a shining heap upon the coarse cloth.

Parson Jones raised both hands into the air, and Tom stared at what he saw, wondering whether it was all so, and whether he was really awake. It seemed to him as though he was in a dream.

There were twenty-two bags in all in the chest; ten of them full of silver money, eight of them full of gold money, three of them full of gold dust, and one small bag with jewels wrapped up in cotton and paper.

"'Tis enough," cried out Parson Jones, "to make us both rich men as long as we live."

About Michael Hague

Michael Hague's first book, a pop-up version of *Gulliver in Lilliput*, was published by Hallmark Cards in 1975. Michael has since become the renowned illustrator of numerous children's classics, including *The Rainbow Fairy Book*, a collection of thirty-one traditional fairy tales edited by Andrew Lang, as well as his own collections, *The Book of Dragons* and *The Book of Fairies*. His work as an artist enables him to "be like Peter Pan and never grow up." He says, "Being able to make pictures for all the books that were my childhood friends is like being in Never-Never Land. I not only paint fairy tales; I get to live one."

Michael lives with his wife, Kathleen, a frequent collaborator, and their family in Colorado Springs, Colorado.